LOST AND FOUND
IN THE 60S

a novel by Paul Justison

To Ann Justison, my first love. I remember the freedom and joy we shared, as well as my regrets.

To those who suffered through early drafts but still encouraged me – Bruce Gurganus, Caroline Arnold, David Silva, Ezra Gould, Geneva Ulm, Jean-Luc Szpakowski, Laura Grandin, Les Cordoza, Linda Hopkins, Martha Kearns, Michelle Silver, Norah Booth, Patricia Steward, and Peter Chartrand.

James Fadiman both boosted my spirits with his kudos and took the time to convince me that the original ending had to be changed.

I want to thank *The Rumpus* which published an abridged version of the first chapter, *April 1968* in 2016; and www.fictionontheweb.co.uk, which published the second chapter, *Tucson, 1966*, in 2021.

This novel would not have been published without my editors - Jessica Levine and Ann Ireland – who persuaded me that my long-ago advanced college English classes did not mean my grammar was word perfect.

I thank the folks at Unsolicited Press, in particular S.R. Stewart, Gage Greenspan, Robin LeeAnn, and Kathryn Gerhardt.

My children – Patrick Justison, Kate Arnold, Liz Justison, and Marcelle Havens - encouraged me along the way, especially Kate who read multiple early drafts.

I want to thank my wife, lover, and friend Karen Saeger, who eagerly read and edited. Most of all, she kept challenging me to stretch myself to improve a scene, to bring a character to vivid life, and to keep the readers perspective in mind. She did not live through those sixties, but she helped me bring them alive.

Contents

"The trick is growing up without growing old."

Casey Stengel

Lost And Found
In The 60s

April 1968

Tony and I went out delivering late one spring morning. As we reached Oak Street, Janis Joplin drove by in a convertible, hair all over and waving to people she'd pick out. "I've never seen her in that car. What is it?" I asked.

Tony knew cars. "A Nash Metropolitan. Don't think they make them anymore."

"We should see her again."

"Absolutely man, 'Ball and Chain.'" He walked down Oak, on his route. My first two stops were uneventful, and I continued around Buena Vista Park for the last of the day.

Jerry let me into the two-story Victorian he shared with his old lady, Connie. His parents had died and left him the house and not much else. After finishing college in Maine, he started his mail-order business with a clientele of friends back East, buying small lots of acid.

They had a workroom in the basement stocked with different sized boxes, wrapping materials, and all sorts of stuff from thrift shops—hats, photos, books, kitchen things, etc.—to add to the boxes. Some they'd wrap as presents; the rest just had brown paper. They'd address them from legitimate addresses in the city and drop them off at post offices near that address or somewhere downtown.

Months ago, I'd told Connie I was paranoid that she'd send one from the home address of one of the mail handlers, and they'd catch it. They switched to only using expensive addresses.

I liked both of them but never figured out how they were an item. Jerry always looked close to straight—brown hair barely over his ears and a clean-shaven, serious face, not too unlike me in that regard. But he was close to homely with bushy eyebrows and a chin that never quite separated from his neck. Connie was one foxy lady, green eyes always sizing up whether you were enough for her. Last I saw her, she was wearing a black and red plaid skirt, purplish tights, and black boots. But she wasn't here today.

Jerry had news for me. "Mark, we're quitting all this at the end of summer. Connie and I are going to law school. We were accepted last week."

It was a shock to me. But we made arrangements for next time, and I left, wondering how I'd replace them. They were a reliable quarter of the business.

Tony was at the Here and Now, this macrobiotic place he liked on Haight at Scott. There was never much choice for lunch, so I ordered brown rice with squash and an apple juice.

I asked, "Do we come here because they don't have the food you don't like or because they have the food you do like?"

He grinned before turning serious. "I never see straight people here, loud people, or smelly people. Just people devoted to macrobiotics. And us."

It wasn't bad today; they hadn't turned the squash to mush.

"Connie and Jerry are quitting in July or August."

Tony wasn't concerned. "Don't worry. We've replaced people before."

"But this is different. They're our most reliable people."

"I know a couple who want in. You can meet them, and we'll talk. We have time."

He was right. We had time, plenty of time. What neither of us mentioned was what we had even more of now—risk. Having to replace someone added an extra layer on top of all the other everyday risks we had to keep our eyes and ears open for.

After we finished lunch, we stashed our cash at our flats and headed back to the street. All sorts of people visited the Haight, most with no intention of staying long. Today, one group interested us—college chicks on break. Some had boys with them, but many were unchaperoned. They came in twos, threes, or fours. They drove from Oregon, Colorado, Washington, Michigan, Ohio, and once (most delightfully) Kansas. They came curious about the Haight, about hippies, about a world away from white bread, and most of them, even if they wouldn't say it, came looking for drugs and sex.

Most visitors in cars drove either up Haight or up Masonic and turned onto Haight. We'd hang out in a strategic spot, catch the gossip, and observe the cars with out-of-state plates. If they turned us on, we'd follow, hoping they were looking for a parking spot. Today, a Jeep from Montana drove by and parked near the Straight Theater, but they gave us an odd look, and it wasn't worth the effort to change their minds. Then a Volvo with Wisconsin plates and two chicks of definite interest went by and turned right on Stanyan. We lost sight of them when they turned again, but we hustled and saw them parallel parking on the Panhandle side of Oak. As we reached them, they were stowing things in the trunk. They had sense enough to lock things out of sight but didn't have street antennae to catch us approaching.

Tony asked, "Did you drive all the way from Madison, or you going to Berkeley?"

They looked us up and down and smiled with none of that uptight East Coast stuff. The blond answered with wide lips and an almost goofy grin. "Madison. Stayed in Reno last night."

I asked the obvious and unthreatening, "Came to see the Haight?"

"We'd heard it had gone downhill, but we wanted to see it anyway. And there's a Quicksilver concert tonight." She looked at her brown-haired friend and then back at us. "I'm Emma, and this is Irene."

"I'm Mark, and this ugly guy is Tony."

Emma defended him. "He's not ugly."

One issue was out of the way; we knew who'd go with Tony. I pulled out a joint. "Bet you didn't get a chance to smoke on the trip."

Dark-haired Irene replied with the suggestion of a smile, "No, and Madison's been dry." I could like her: her confidence, her angular face, and her serene eyes.

We found a grassy spot in the Panhandle and lit up. We'd been getting our weed lately from two North Beach chicks, who must have taken lessons from Cubans because they rolled these sweet, evenly burning joints. There were different kinds of weed, almost all made you hungry. Most worked on your head and made you think you were the brightest cat in the universe, which just made things more exciting or worse, made you paranoid. Some weed worked on your body and mellowed you out. The chicks separated theirs as best they could into their mind-blowing joints and their mellow joints. The mellow ones put a governor on my normally racing mind, letting me notice small treasures. This was definitely mellow.

We sat cross-legged, sharing the joint, while the fog and the sun randomly shared the sky. A little breeze kept flitting through Irene's hair. The little tufts around her ears had a curl that gave me shivers. She took off her jacket, and the tiny hairs on her arms moved just ever so. When the joint was gone, I settled back on my side toward her. She stretched out her long legs and leaned back, resting her upper body on her forearms without moving any further from me—maybe even an inch closer.

Tony said, "Mark's favorite band is Quicksilver. Think we could go with you tonight?"

The girls glanced at each other and smiled at us. Emma asked, "We could, but where do you guys live? In the Haight?"

Tony pointed out our building on Fell and told them about Lagunitas, building it up with the solitude of the forest, the fresh air, and Big Brother and the Holding Company having lived there before us.

The girls took in Tony's answer and smiled, relaxing into the calm of the pot. Then Emma stood up and shook her hair all around. Her blue eyes sparkled as she said, "I feel like running." And she did, down the Panhandle and toward Masonic with Tony chasing and Irene and I following. At Masonic, we grouped up and went on a tour of the Haight. Recent arrivals asked for spare change. Street dealers eyed us. Local cats and chicks hustled along to get off the street.

Unwelcome overnight smells mixed with oversweet incense. A tour bus rolled along, bulging with camera-snapping voyeurs.

When Emma and Irene had had enough of the street, we went to our building. They wanted to know what to wear, and Tony said, "Something colorful." Emma put on leather boots, a red and black exploding African dress, and a big coat with a furry collar. Sort of the hip African tundra look. Irene had slipped into tight jeans and a purple turtleneck. A knit sweater balanced on one shoulder.

I said, "We can take two cars or go all together in one if you want." I didn't want to take two, but it was better to let them decide.

Irene didn't look at Emma, just at me, with a new and stimulating smirk. "Let's take one." We ate dinner at a seafood place on Polk Street and then walked to the Avalon on Van Ness for the concert. Some dealers hung out with the bands, giving the stuff away for a chance to bang the groupies and bask in the fame. Too high profile for us. We paid our way in.

Used to see lots of psychedelic princes and princesses on Haight Street. Not many these days. They stayed away from the street as much as possible. But here were hundreds of the turned on and tuned in, dressed like birds and peacocks in heat. Tony and I did our part. He wore black-and-white striped pants and a big-collared purple shirt. I was sedate with dark blue plush pants, a collarless striped shirt, and a red plaid cap.

Inside, we breathed in the music of the first band. Irene didn't want to dance, so she and I went up on the balcony to watch the bands and the pride of the counterculture. I had long since dropped the teenage reluctance to put a protective arm around a girl, but you had to pick your moments. Twice, I held back with Irene. Wasn't sure why until I realized she reminded me more of a girl I'd rather forget than anyone else I'd ever met. Had to break through that barrier. I draped an arm around her shoulders, hand and fingers spread along her upper arm. I got a smile and forgot all about Clare.

Quicksilver grabbed our attention with 'Who do you Love.' The first few notes kick-started your bass inner drive and then the rhythm jumped in. Below us, some danced wildly, but mostly everyone on the floor was in long, ragged lines, facing the stage, swaying, and stomping to the music. Bo Diddly popularized it, but Quicksilver made it into a thrilling sensual swirl that left you needing someone to hold when it was over.

Irene edged closer. "God, I love that song."

"Sure you don't want to go down on the floor?"

Downstairs, we found a place in a line and swayed and swirled until the last chord of the last song. Emma was raring to go to Lagunitas, so we fetched their car to caravan north—Tony and Emma in the Volvo, Irene and me in the Starfire.

On the Golden Gate, Irene wanted to look at the ocean, so I hugged the row of orange cones separating traffic. Still, I don't think she could have seen much of it with the bridge all lit up. We headed up Highway 101 and west out on Sir Francis Drake. In America, you got roads named after you if you were an English knight, even a bloodthirsty slaver and pirate. The road made a big left in front of the Orange Julius, with its concoctions of mystery orange flavoring, dairy residue, and ice—the stoners' cure for macrobiotic ills and smokers' throats. If the local narcs had any cultural understanding, they'd stake out the Orange Julius and grab the entire stoner population of Marin in a week.

"What do you two do?" Irene asked as we headed up the hills outside of Fairfax.

"Sociological fieldwork on the revolutionary aspects of psychedelia and sex."

"What do you really do?"

"How about revolutionary entrepreneurs specializing in psychedelia?"

"Emma and I let ourselves be picked up by two dealers?"

I couldn't see her face very well in this light, but she didn't sound indignant. "Two thoroughly groovy and charming ones."

"I can see that." She ran her hands through her hair, releasing a bouquet of sweet flowers and vanilla. "Could we stop before we get to your place?"

"Sure, but there isn't much open but McAuliffe's Pub."

"I don't need anything. I just want to talk."

She's got cold feet. Damn! I passed the pub and pulled into the post office lot.

Her face turned to me. She asked, "Do you pick up a lot of girls?"

"Only when I see one I'm really attracted to…"

"How often is that?"

"Well, not every day…"

I saw her face in the headlights of a passing car. She was praying in the young women's church of controlled sensuality.

"Tell me why you like me."

"I like the way you are quiet and speak confidently. You're assured about yourself and just controlled enough to go about wisely in this world." Did she move slightly closer? "I like your serene dark eyes, the way the little hairs move around your ears, and the way you tilt your head slightly when you're thinking. And Irene sounds so sweet. Eye…reen, eye…reen. The vanilla in your hair is pulling me toward you."

A most welcome smile. "Let's see the lodge."

The Starfire responded to my foot, and I caressed the steering wheel around the curves and hills until we parked behind the Wisconsin Volvo. "I have the cabin out back."

"Let's see it."

Thankfully, I'd left the place neat and had made the bed. Hell, I'd even shaken out my rugs. "There's no heat, but it's warm under the covers."

"Don't worry. I'm from Wisconsin."

She wasn't cold, but she stood by the door, looking around at my chair and my writing desk. More second thoughts? I sure didn't want to say good night. I had to jump into the breach. Took off my jacket and undid the buttons on my shirt one at a time until her eyes said keep going.

***

The next day, the Wisconsinites, Tony, and I dropped a full tab each with our lodge mates, Rachel and Danny, watching over us. Tony and Emma took blankets into the woods, and we didn't see them until the next day. Irene wanted to stay out on our big deck under the canopy of pine trees, so I brought out a quilt and pillows.

She stretched out those long legs and propped herself on an elbow, her head toward me, blinking as the sun moved through the clouds. She'd put on the olive work shirt an old girlfriend had given me. Months ago, I wouldn't have let anybody wear it, but it looked fine on Irene, especially with the rolled-up sleeves exposing the little hairs on her forearms.

I asked, "Can I see your foot?"

"My foot?" She laughed. "Which one?"

"The left."

Her sock and boot off, I caressed her strong lean ankle and massaged her arch. Kissed her toes until she laughed. Released her foot and stretched out next to her. "Were you a ballerina?"

"A mouse."

"A mouse?"

"In the Nutcracker."

"Dance for me, little mouse?"

She absorbed my request pore by pore, the acid opening up all the geography of her brain. Her words rolled out as she stood. "Limber up with me!"

Mimicked her stretches. Sunlight rippled off our bodies. Acid pumping, pulsating through flexing limbs. She danced. Enthralled and trying to follow, I tripped, clattering to the deck. She radiated smiles and danced around me.

Irene. I. R.E.N.E. Letters bursting in the air as she sat. I saw her heart pumping. Red, red, deep red. Pumping, pumping, outside her body. I stopped breathing, almost panicking, but she touched me. Touched me, and I breathed again. Slow and deep, breathing again.

Rachel appeared on the deck by the window. Then she was next to us, freckles dropping all over."Muffins…and…lemonade…for…you." She sat down a tray. "Muffins…are…warm. Warm."

Irene watched Rachel leave, turned, and looked through me to the other side. My hands wrapped around a cool, moist mug and put it to her lips. She sipped. Her eyes opened so wide, her face disappeared. Lemon trees danced all around. Rippling sunlight flashing off yellow fruit.

A muffin wouldn't let me take it. I got down, eyeball to muffin, staring at it while it glared back at me. Irene's hand flashed and took it. "Wow!"

She put some in my mouth. Warm and crumbly. My tongue moved it all around, and I breathed again.

I spread out, flat on the deck. Soft guitar notes tickled me. Irene's head on my chest.

She moved away, and my heart revved like an engine. Held it in my chest and a big red and white sign said stop. Oh, Irene. Irene.

Lost in swirls. Fading…dozing…

Felt my shoulder under blankets. Words appeared at my ear. Hair tickling. Body moving.

"It's…getting…cold." Rachel's face spilling sounds. "Let's get up…and go inside."

Rachel and Irene way, way up there.

Feet strong, attaching and holding onto the deck. Grabbed the light every step to the lodge. Every small step. The door, still the tree it was, looked at me and yielded to my muscle.

Inside, angry old trees threw out sparks from the big stones, and the light flashed off Irene. She was warm. Oh, so warm. I shook and released. Released some more.

Rachel appeared, carrying bowls with magic steam. Happy seeds ran around green and yellow chunks on top of hundreds of brown, pulsing bits. We ate with teeth avoiding tongues. Chests warming. Bellies calming.

Fat glass with juicy red on the table. "I brought you wine. Small sips. Small."

Irene's hand rippled to the wine. She drank, and her body jiggled all the way back to the sofa.

I let my hand go to hers and wrapped it around the glass. She smiled at me, and I took it, lips puckering and raspberry jammy wine sluicing through me.

Rachel, Mother Rachel. "Let's go to your cabin." She walked us over, gave us water, and closed the door. We dissolved into each other under all the blankets.

***

Awoke into Irene's dreamy gaze. Smiled from inside and felt her leg astride me. I wouldn't need much in this world if she'd just keep looking at me like that.

Her lips moved. "Hungry?" She broke her own spell.

I found cereal and milk in the kitchen and brought it to the cabin. Refreshed, we took a walk through the cool, chattering forest.

"So, what can you do other than deal?"

"I'm good in bed."

"I already know that, Romeo."

"Used to write poetry and read at recitals, but I stopped and threw away what I'd written."

"Why?"

"Lost my muse." Almost said, "There's an opening." But then Clare came to my mind. Clare and her earnestness, her loose hairs by her ears. Clare and her betrayal.

Irene interrupted my mixed-up memory and asked, "So, who did you like?"

Glad for her question but couldn't really focus. "Whitman, Rimbaud, Cummings. You?"

"I read *Howl* because of the controversy, and I've read some Sandburg. Physics majors don't get to read a lot of poetry."

"A physicist. Impressive!"

She found a flat, smooth tree stump and sat. Knees pulled up and hands pressed into the stump near her hips.

I stretched out on some leaves.

"I'm not a physicist yet, but I want to be one even more now. You work on these problems, and they are all so abstract and mathematical. Then yesterday happened. There was time, and then there was no time. Fast time and slow time. The light was expanding and shrinking and switching colors. Then space… I can't even formulate what I felt and saw."

I wish I knew something about physics. Anything to talk about with her. An idea almost formed in my mind when she slid off the stump and lay alongside me, face-to-face. "I'm so glad I could do it with you, in this place and with people to watch out for us."

Now, I didn't know what to say at all. Didn't know what to say because I felt something for her. No mistake. It was there. Hadn't happened in so long. I wanted to reach out and hold her, just hold her. Did I want to ask her how she felt about me? My heart accelerated, and I didn't know what to do.

Tony and Emma interrupted my indecision. "Hey, we're going to the beach. Come with us."

The moment lost. Was I sad or relieved—or both?

We picnicked at Stinson Beach before Irene and Emma headed back to Wisconsin. Irene gave me a warm goodbye but never offered her address. I didn't feel comfortable asking for it and knew I'd have to clean up my act before I could have a woman like her.

Tucson, 1966

My inner clock had beaten the alarm by almost four minutes. Not sure why I even set the thing. Safety, maybe. Dressed and opened the door of my sanctuary. Quiet in the rest of the trailer, and I kept it that way, eating a bowl of Rice Chex. Avoided Mother's heels and a pair of boots in the living room, shut the door behind me, and strode out of the Oasis for Mobile Living.

Often, on the way to school, I'd glimpse at the mountains ringing the town and remember peaceful walks in their shelter. Sometimes, I'd picture what else surrounded Tucson—Titan intercontinental ballistic missiles. We could destroy eighteen Soviet cities with the nine-megaton nuclear warhead on each Titan. Our annihilation would occur with the initial Soviet strike or from the resulting fallout. I never worried which.

A modern architect designed Javelina High with bold shapes and real curves. They could hold geometry class while touring the buildings. The school board wouldn't hire him again, though. All the curves offended their stiff minds. I should know. At a dance junior year, they suspended a girl and me for doing the two-step too close. I was positive our chests or hips never touched; I would have known. But those curves had to be kept from contact. The shape alone was enough to offend.

First class after lunch was chemistry with Mr. Boone. He had a puffy face and thin lips that he was reluctant to part. As

I finished today's experiment and cleaned my work area, a classmate came over and said, "Mark, the principal wants you."

"What for?"

He shrugged and lowered his eyes. Delivering messages to the school's rebel with or without a cause was probably not a task he'd volunteered for, so I nodded and got off my stool. Eyes around the benches rose. Mr. Boone sat motionless, face averted and hands out of sight.

I gave my lab book a gentle toss, plopping on his desk. "My book, Mr. Boone." I sauntered out of the classroom and over to the lobby of the main building where big globes dangled from the ceiling. Disneyland was our nickname, but I liked plain old Javelina High and our prophylactic mascot, the Trojans.

Mrs. Apariencia stood behind the counter in Administration. A flip curl in her hair and a light blue sweater with only the top button closed.

"What's this all about Mrs. A.?" I asked. She didn't belong here. She actually cared about students.

"I don't know, but they've been in there a while." She nodded toward the principal's office. "Whatever is happening, remember, you have scholarships waiting."

Dean Gall interrupted. "Mr. Stenrud, please come in."

I entered the principals' den—photos on the walls, trophies in a cabinet, and hardly a book. Four of them—Principal Piltz behind his desk, two deans on a divan, and my track coach in a chair. Someone from a different planet or continent would have a hard time telling them apart—Anglo, buzz cut, short-sleeved white shirts, and clip-on ties.

Dean Gall began the inquisition. "Mark, this is serious. We cannot allow students to disobey their teachers."

"Okay. What's this have to do with me?"

Gall had the pinkest face of the four. "Don't play games with us."

"I'm not. Please, tell me why I'm here." Had someone blamed something on me?

Principal Piltz couldn't wait to take over. "Mark, we know what happened. Mr. Boone asked you to remove your pin, and you refused."

"He didn't even speak to me today, and he sure didn't ask me to take off my pin." I usually wore two or three anti-war pins. Today, I just had on my USSR — Hungary 1956 / USA — Vietnam 1966 pin. I'd taken a liking to it after I'd read a paperback, Mother's latest had left lying around. The cover featured a beautiful Hungarian named Ilona wearing black and Sandor, a kid my age, holding a smoking machine gun. During the Hungarian uprising, Sandor shot Soviets and threw Molotov cocktails, while Ilona taught him all about what women want. She certainly taught him more than any kid at Javelina High knew.

"Mark, are you with us? We're talking about your pins."

I snapped back. "I wasn't asked to take this pin off, and I don't see why I should."

"Are you accusing Mr. Boone of lying to us?"

"Why isn't he here?"

Piltz came around his desk and stopped in front of my chair, towering over me. "Mark, we are deeply concerned that your pins are creating an unsafe condition for our students."

"They're pins, not bombs."

"They could lead to violence. You'll have to stop wearing them if you are to remain at Javelina High."

I was surprised by this ridiculous demand, but years of Mother's training kicked in—breath slowing, senses on alert. "This is totally wrong. I wear pins to protest our inhumane assault on the Vietnamese people. We have freedom of speech. We have elections for class offices—young Republicans, young Democrats—and you want me to stop wearing my pins?"

"This is not a debate. You'll stop wearing them, or you'll be suspended." Piltz caught himself and reduced his glare. "Mark, we think it best for you to go home for the rest of the day. You'll have the weekend to think things over. There'll be no penalty for missing your remaining classes."

I didn't know what to say, so I stood. They weren't ready for that, so I left with my tiny victory of surprise.

Mrs. A. wasn't behind the counter. I marched out of campus and down Dodge Boulevard for three-fifths of a mile. No sidewalk, just dirt and gravel. No trees, just telephone and utility poles. I didn't stop until I crossed Grant Road and reached the Oasis.

Our little lot was in the first row I'd come to. Mother's car was gone, and I went inside the trailer. Left my books in my room and went back outside to the cinder block temple of hygiene. The male side had four showers, toilets, sinks with mirrors, and electrical outlets. I guessed the female side was similar. Trailer parks had their pecking orders; those without plumbing were at the bottom and had some stigma attached for using the communal showers. I didn't mind though. In fact, I preferred leaving our bathroom to Mother and enjoying the torrential water pressure in the communal blockhouse.

The shower faucets released their elixir from high up on the wall. I stood upright, imagining a glorious waterfall. Cool water cascading over smooth rocks, spray all around. The fast, smooth liquid worked for a time, keeping the shameful prospect of not wearing my pins out of my mind, but the administrators' faces kept coming back. I couldn't let them win.

I changed in the trailer, used my fingers as a comb, slung my corduroy sport coat over my left shoulder, and ventured out for the night's poetry reading. The university was about three miles away, less than forty minutes with my long legs and easy stride. I could take a bus, but there were better uses for my cash. Besides, there was a cool November breeze. I avoided main streets with cars screeching, squealing, and honking and tailpipes releasing. Avoided the signs selling, stores purveying, and eyes judging. Angled instead through quiet residential streets

The reading was in a redbrick Unitarian church. I'd toured it a month before and was amazed there was no confessional. I realized then why nuns had taught us it was a sin to visit churches of other religions. They didn't want you to learn that you didn't need a priest in a box for forgiveness.

As I reached the church, I saw two people I'd met at the last reading across the street. The guy called to me, and I went over to them. "Remember us," he said. "I'm Chas, and this is Terry." He had an easy smile, and his brown hair fell over his ears and onto the collar of his army surplus jacket. Terry was far more interesting—hands hard in the pockets of her open navy pea coat, lean face untouched by makeup.

"You two going to the reading? I have some new poems."

Terry shook her ponytail, blue eyes sparkling in the streetlights. "It's canceled. They put up a sign yesterday."

"What a drag!"

They whispered something, and Chas asked, "You smoke weed?"

I smiled.

Terry took a step forward. "My little sister, Lauren, is here from Scottsdale for the weekend. I'm not setting up a date or anything, but we're going to a party tonight, and I don't want the college boys hitting on her. Would you come along?"

"Sure, but will she want to?"

Terry laughed. "She's a high school senior too, and you're, well, you're…" Her smile grew. "It'll work out."

Chas had a car I'd never seen before—a Citroën—plush inside and roomy enough for my lanky body in the backseat. We stopped at a two-story Spanish-style house, and Terry brought out her sister. Blond hair shorter than I'd ever seen on a girl, revealing a high forehead and giving me a start. Her flared nose was set at the barest angle, which made her all the more exciting. She sat a little stiffly. A jerk of the steering wheel or a big bump could send her right on top of me. At least, so I was hoping.

It must have been five minutes before she spoke. "So, what's the surprise? Where we're going? Or is it him?"

Terry looked back at her sister. "I told you at the house. We know Mark from the poetry readings. He has a great voice, and he makes the poems come alive."

Lauren finished assessing me and asked, "Great voice? You looking at a career in local radio?"

I couldn't tell if she was being sarcastic or just playful. "Maybe, if I can pick the music."

"You into surfer music?" she asked.

"No, not really. I like the Stones a lot, the Byrds, and the Who."

She relaxed and sank back into the seat. "Sing something with me."

"I'm not very good at singing."

"C'mon, 'You Can't Hurry Love.' Sing it with me!"

"Really, I can't sing." Wasn't sure I remembered the words either.

"Come on!"

I couldn't resist her smile, and we sang a few verses.

Terry turned back to us. "Hey, you two, you're ruining the song."

Lauren landed an easy punch on my shoulder. "You're right. You can't sing at all." She moved closer and then asked the front seat, "Where are you taking us?"

Terry said, "To Nogales. To a Tokeathon."

Chas asked, "Have you been to one in Mexico?"

We each said no, and I didn't volunteer the fact that I hadn't even been to a domestic Tokeathon.

Terry studied us while Chas drove and talked. "We've got three cars. One's getting the brick. One's bringing drinks, and we're buying food. We're all meeting up on a hill outside of town. We have one important rule. Never put any weed in your pockets. They could search us going home. Got it?"

Lauren and I chorused, "Okay."

Chas said, "We're going to stop for munchies before we cross the border."

Being fond of Mexican bakeries, I asked, "Why don't we get pastries on the other side?"

"You speak Spanish?"

"Enough to buy pastries."

Terry handed me a ten. "There could be fourteen of us. Is that enough?"

"More than."

We had to wait at the border with all the Friday night traffic, but when we pulled up to the Mexican checkpoint, they just waved us through. Chas didn't take the easy way out of town, heading down the main business street instead. Shops specializing in gallons and half gallons of tequila, rum, and any other salable variety of liquor outnumbered the craft, leather, and clothing stores. Cheap booze brought the masses across the border.

We found a large panaderia with hundreds of sweet baked goodies neatly arranged in four glass display cases. A nice old lady, who didn't look like she enjoyed too many of her own pastries, boxed up an assortment of three dozen with some of my favorites: empanadas de pina and conos.

After I paid, a man in a gray suit spoke to me in Spanish. I asked him to repeat it. He did, and I still didn't get it, at which point most of the shop tried to suppress their giggles and laughs. The man got a little red in the face. But he recovered and said in English, "I'm sorry, young man. I didn't want to embarrass you, but I was complimenting you on your Spanish." I mumbled something, shook his hand, and pondered the problem of knowing only part of something.

With our shopping finished, Chas found the fast road out, and we headed south and then east. Houses grew further and further apart, and the naked, solitary light bulbs burning outside almost every front door cast less and less light on the hills. Soon, the barking of chained dogs gave way to the howling of coyotes, and Chas turned off the main road and up into the hills, stopping next to a VW bug and an old milk delivery truck. We found the others up on a small plateau, and Chas introduced me and Lauren. A tall, broad-shouldered guy named Peter gave us the same rules and said we'd have to do the seeding and stemming because we were first-timers.

He took us to a flat area, where a brick of weed wrapped in orange cellophane rested on newspaper. I'd never seen one before. It was maybe four inches by eight by twelve. He broke off a chunk of compressed stems, buds, and leaves, releasing a sweet, earthy scent. He showed us how to clean it and left us to the task after rolling a few joints. Lauren gathered the buds, and I began the finger-scratching task of separating weed from seeds and stems.

Peter came back after we'd cleaned a fair amount and lit a joint for us. I asked him, "Are we going to smoke all of this?"

"No way!" He laughed. "We've got a connection who gives a good price on a brick. Sometimes, he'll sell half. Even with a full brick, it's cheaper and safer than buying smaller on the street."

I wasn't sure I understood, but I let it go, and he left with the buds and loose weed. We relaxed, looking at the stars while the others hung out nearby, smoking and laughing.

"You going steady?" she asked.

"No, you?"

All I got was a sarcastic laugh, and we went back to cleaning. Peter reappeared with another guy and said we'd done enough. He gave us a joint the size of a small cigar. "Once you get it going, just take little puffs. There's juice and soda over there with those pastries you brought. We don't have any blankets. We don't want any weed getting caught on them."

As they were leaving, the other guy stared at Lauren, probably at her short hair. She turned her head and looked down. Her lips pursed.

I wanted to move closer but wasn't sure. Instead, I asked, "You okay?"

Her shoulders eased, and she turned to me. "What do you think of my hair?"

I didn't think, just said, "I like it because it lets me see all of your face."

She smiled. "No one has ever said that."

"Can I run my fingers through it?"

"Maybe."

I reached partway, hand suspended inches from my target, but she pushed it away and held out the cigar-sized joint. "I want to light it, but I'm cold."

I moved closer until we were shoulder to shoulder, hip to hip. Got up the courage and started to put my arm around her, but she turned her face to me and back so fast that I hesitated.

Time went by as her magnetic field kept pulling me, while I reluctantly resisted, unsure and uncertain. Then I felt her arm around me. Relieved, I put mine just above hers, and we stargazed for a while. Most delightfully, she rested her head on my shoulder.

Terry came over. "You two okay?"

Lauren looked up and said, "We're fine."

Terry said, "Those pastries are really, really, absolutely good." She jumped up a foot or so. "Yeah… They're…they're really good. Absolutely…far-out good." She walked and jumped off.

"My big sister is really…really…absolutely stoned." We laughed, and Lauren pointed to the colossal joint. I got it going, and we toked for a while. Legs intertwined and arms wrapped around each other, we switched from star gazing to face gazing.

Chas plopped down next to us. "Hey, you two, I brought pastries and juice."

I didn't realize how stoned I was until I looked at Chas and tried to speak.

He saw me trying to talk, grinned, and said, "Nothing in your pockets." He headed back to the group.

Lauren found my lips with hers. Our senses doubly alive from the weed, hit high registers of whoopee. Kisses lingered, triply amplified with the palate twisting tastes of juice, pineapple pastry, and crème-filled cone.

Peter came over with another guy, who asked, "Hey man, those pastries…those pastries. They were like out…out of this fucking world. You got any more?"

"No. I brought them all up."

He bit his lip and walked around in little circles.

Peter asked, "You need any more weed?"

"No, we're fine."

"We'll be heading out in a while."

They left, and we went back to face gazing and kissing until my inner clock interfered, and I asked, "Maybe we should test our legs."

"I want you next to me."

"We could walk around together."

"You just want to show me off!"

"Yes, I do!"

She smiled and lurched up, me following. She fell back, and I caught her, but I lost my balance and landed flat with Lauren on top of me, face-to-face.

"You did that on purpose," she said.

"No, but I liked it." I felt something pointed beneath my back. "I have to get up. I'm lying on rocks." We gathered our debris and shambled over to a small, freshly dug garbage pit. We dumped our trash and joined our companions in cross-border enlightenment by the cars. A tall redhead, hair tumbling out of her watch cap, said, "Listen up, you dope fiends. We don't want to go over the border together, so we'll draw straws."

Chas got the short straw, and we had to wait twenty minutes. We stood by the Citroën, checking out the stars and shaking out our limbs until Terry asked, "Say Mark, can we get something to eat on this side of the border instead of waiting here?"

"I know a place."

Cool wind rushed in and out of the open car windows, dispelling our rich aroma until we slowed, entering back into town. After a few turns, we saw the neon sign—Bar de la Prensa. Inside, five men sat at the bar. Only one turned to look at us. A waiter gave us a table in a corner, and I ordered from the small menu—fruit drinks and plates of eggs with machaca. We were the only gringos, but we weren't drunk and loud, and nobody but the waiter paid us any attention. Even so, we were all a little zoned and could've gotten paranoid, but the food came, and we started with curious appetites. Hyperactive taste buds mapped the contrasts of moist but charred beef with chilies and tomatoes, creamy eggs, and hot tortillas—every distinct flavor pleasantly amplified. As we finished, we pushed back our chairs, satisfied and softly stoned.

Chas looked around and asked, "How'd you find this place?"

"You used to be able to bring back a gallon of liquor for every person in a car, so grown-ups would bring kids along to get more booze. A friend's dad liked to eat here. I liked coming with him. He'd teach us Spanish to pass the time on the drive."

The waiter brought the bill, and I started to contribute, but Chas looked at the number and waved me off. Back in the car, he said, "They could take us inside and search us at the border, but we're okay because we've got nothing. The smell should even be gone by now. And I'm the only guy with long hair, so just look straight."

At the checkpoint, Chas answered a few questions from the border agent, who looked us over and seemed puzzled by Lauren's short hair, but he let us through.

Terry let out a rush of air and said, "That was the easiest time we've had in a while."

Chas said, "Maybe he went on average hair length."

Terry looked startled for a moment and then changed the subject. "Mark, where are we dropping you off back in Tucson?"

I was about to answer when Lauren leaned toward her sister. "We're not dropping him anywhere. He's staying with me."

Chas kept his eyes on the road but offered some helpful insight. "Terry, no one could get a putty knife between those two tonight."

She shrugged and laid her head on his shoulder. Lauren slid next to me, gave a dreamy look, and drifted off, her arms and legs corralling me.

I had expected to be dropped off, likely arranging to meet again, so I was overcome with joy and shock when Lauren claimed me for the night. Never felt like that before. My eyes wide open, basking in Lauren's glow and the receding pot. Memories of my other sad experiences tried to invade, but her warmth kept them away.

Inside their Tucson house, Terry took Lauren into another room, and I followed Chas into the kitchen. Dishes, glasses, and supplies stood neatly behind the glass of wood cabinets. Windows over the sink looked out into a side yard.

He poured glasses of cold water and gave me a big one-armed hug. He said something, but I barely heard him, focusing instead on trying to remember the bedroom lessons Ilona had given Sandor in my Hungarian novel.

Lauren found me in the kitchen and tugged me toward the stairs. She went up two at a time, and I did the same. In her bedroom, she opened the French doors' blinds, starlight spreading across an unmade bed.

We stood staring at each other in the striped cosmic rays. I was frozen, standing by her bed, but I watched her face go through the same emotions until magic intervened. We held each other and kissed. Stripped off our jackets and stumbled into bed as if we were still on the rocky hill. Got warm, arms around, holding and caressing, and legs intertwined. Exploring lips banished fear and memories. We linked at the hip, two halves of a bicycle sprocket going through the gears—climbing, racing, coasting, climbing again, and gliding on into glorious sleep.

***

Next morning, Lauren drove her sister's Austin-Healey, but she wasn't too smooth with the clutch. "Don't say anything," she said as the car lurched into second. "Don't say anything!"

"I didn't."

"You were about to."

"I'm just watching you because I like watching you."

"So, why do you want a work shirt?" she asked.

"Because you want to buy me something."

"But why a work shirt?"

"It doesn't cost much, and I have a sudden need for one."

"What's the sudden need?"

"I'm going to be suspended from school if I don't stop wearing my peace buttons, and I want to do something different to drive them crazy."

"So, you're going to wear a work shirt?"

"A work shirt and a tie. The young Republicans all wear dress shirts and ties. But what's the difference between a work shirt and a dress shirt?"

She slugged my shoulder. "I like you."

I continued Lauren-gazing until we parked at the army surplus store. She wanted to buy me three or four shirts because they didn't cost much, but I only let her get two roughly textured ones—a light blue and an olive.

She was smoother with the clutch when leaving, but she parked six blocks away in front of a two-story brick house with a large yard and a low plastered wall at the sidewalk. "How many girls have you been with?"

She'd caught me by surprise. "Why are you asking that?"

"I want to know."

Happier than I could remember, but then buried memories sucked out my breath. I felt safe with her, but why was she asking this? I couldn't place the emotion on her face. She wasn't smiling or frowning. Trepidation, was that an emotion? What emotion I had, I didn't know. What I knew was that I couldn't stay in the car's confined space. "Can we sit over there?" I didn't wait for an answer, just got out and sat on the low wall.

Lauren said, "All right, we're here now."

I looked at her, at my knees, and back at her and felt that maybe I could tell someone who'd given me such joy. But I looked back at the sky, trying to avoid her question. She nudged up against me. A dam broke somewhere inside, and I just blurted it out. "Before last night, I'd only been with two, and I've never told anybody about this." Looked at my knees some more. "The first was a big woman. She owned a house in Florida that Mother had moved us into. I was fourteen. She raped me."

I raised my eyes to see her reaction. Her look had turned to confusion or shock. Tried to keep my eyes on her but couldn't. I looked at my knees again, at the Austin, and at the clear desert sky. "One afternoon, she and I were alone in the house. I was tall—but not this tall—and pretty skinny. She was large, fat I guess, and tall for a woman. She had me carry something into her bedroom. She pushed me onto the bed and got on top of me.

"Maybe I could have fought my way out from under her, but I didn't. I didn't even think. I just shut down. She took off her bra, and her breasts hung, big and fleshy. She put my hands on them, and I wanted to crawl out of my skin. Kept trying to look at something else, but all she had on her walls were brightly colored dog paintings: hairy dogs, hairless dogs, small dogs, and big dogs. I couldn't focus on them. My mind kept coming back to her and what she was doing to me."

I had all of Lauren's attention. Nothing outside our space on the low wall existed.

"She took…" Unused to tears, I had trouble going on. I couldn't find my refuge, my solace, my numbness.

"You don't have to tell me anymore." She had an arm around me now and tears of her own. "I'm sorry. I didn't know you'd tell me anything like this."

"No, now I have to!" I raised my voice but caught myself. Ran my hands through my hair and rolled my head. "She took off my pants, but I wasn't hard. I'd dream about girls, look at pictures, and get hard, but I didn't then. She licked and kissed my cock. It felt really weird, but she got on top of me and rocked and rocked like I was some dick on a board."

"That bitch!" She was mad, and I liked that.

I couldn't sit in that open-air confessional any longer. Lauren sensed something. She tugged me up, and we walked hand in hand.

"My second was much different. There's a girl at school I've known for a couple of years. We've been friends, and we talk about politics and colleges. We started making out, and then we did it, but it was completely awkward, and I felt odd afterward. I like her a lot, and she really wants to see me, but I just feel uneasy. I don't know what to do." I looked into Lauren's listening eyes. "That's all."

We drove back to her place without words, only freshly dug secrets.

Terry wasn't home, and we went into Lauren's bedroom. Noon light shone through the open French doors. A breeze stirred tall yellow flowers in a red vase.

I felt dirty and wanted to feel clean around Lauren. "I need a shower."

She had a real bathroom like my grandparents. Smooth, almost white tiles, some with sketches of cacti. She followed me into the glass-enclosed shower.

"Soap?" I asked.

She shook her head. "It dries out your skin." She squeezed liquid from a bottle and washed me up and down.

We dried each other off with a big fluffy towel and lay on her bed—me on my back and her head on my chest.

"My sister lied to you a little," she said. "I don't go to school in Scottsdale. I used to, but now I go to a boarding school in Texas."

"Why'd you switch?"

She propped herself up on a bent arm. "It was more than just changing schools. I had a huge fight with my dad and shaved off all my hair. I was so angry with myself and at some boys, and I was ashamed. And everything was…"

She looked away, then back at me, and continued. "I had a sort of boyfriend. We used to make out, and then we did it, but it was like nothing. It wasn't as good as just making out. I tried again with him, but the same thing, nothing. I tried it with others, and the same thing, nothing. Then everybody was talking about me, that I was this horrible slut. Dad's friends found out and then dad… He might have been better if Mom were still alive, but…" She sat up with her eyes still on me. "It was really hard because I know he loves me, but he freaked out. I didn't know what to do. Terry was on a trip. I couldn't talk to her." She closed her eyes. "I flipped out and cut off all my hair. He threatened to send me away to school. I told him, 'Go ahead. Get me out of here.'"

I wanted to make it right but didn't know what to say. All I could do was listen. She wrapped around me, and we lay there as the light retreated across the room.

We didn't hear the car or the front door, but we heard the voice. "Lauren, I'm home."

Downstairs, Terry sat in the living room on a red sofa. Three arched French doors behind her gave a view of the backyard and a wall of white oleander beyond. "You look terrible! Both of you!"

We did look terrible, our faces all tear-streaked.

Lauren sat next to her sister. "Don't worry. We've been talking. We cried a lot too."

"You've been talking all day?"

"Well, we went out to the store, but yeah, we've been here most of the day. I told Mark what happened. All of it. He told me things too. But now we're hungry."

Terry looked at me. "Lauren told you everything, and you're okay with all that?"

"I'm okay with Lauren." I sat down across from Terry.

"And what did you tell Lauren?"

"Personal things."

"And he doesn't have to tell you," Lauren said, "but he understands me."

"Why don't you freshen up and let me talk to Mark?"

"I'm not freshening up. I'm not some freak to talk about when I'm not here."

"I didn't mean anything like that. I just want to talk with Mark."

Lauren said, "Sorry, Terry."

I watched them hug, hug as people who care for each other do. Terry looked at me and then back to her sister.

"Look, you two. I'm responsible here, and I'm probably not doing a very good job. My sister gets her first weekend get-out-of-jail-free card. I set her up with a boy I hardly know but a boy who reads poetry, so I think it'll be safe. And then…" She looked at Lauren and then back toward me. "Mark, I want to know about you."

I told her a lot. Not everything but I didn't hide anything a sister should know. Told her about my parents' divorce, my unusual mother, and my likely scholarships. I said, "Terry, I know you have to look out for Lauren, but I couldn't hurt her. I've been hurt myself. It wasn't what she went through, but I would never… I'm not like that."

Terry looked at us until her own tears started, and she stood. "I have to finish a paper. You two can hang out here or go out, but I have to take Lauren to the airport early tomorrow morning."

We went out. Lauren offered me the keys to the Austin, but I selfishly declined. Watching her was far more pleasurable than paying attention to the road. We parked in the empty bank lot across from the Oasis for Mobile Living.

"Which one's yours?" she asked.

I pointed. "I won't be long, just long enough to change."

"Please, I want to come with you. It doesn't bother me what it is. I just want to see."

"If I were certain Mother wasn't there, sure, but I'm not, and I don't want you to go through what might happen. She's a certified witch."

I entered the trailer as silently as James Bond entering an enemy compound. Put the new work shirts away and changed into jeans and an Oxford shirt.

We ate at El Dorado on South Fourth. It was mostly a pool hall and bar, but the food in the restaurant was tasty and cheap—chile relleno for Lauren and a chimichanga for me. Mid-bite of the crunchy, deep-fried burro, I was struck by the change in my life. Before yesterday, my sensory joys had been quite limited, but looking at Lauren enjoying her stuffed green chile, I realized my pleasures had been multiplied by some factor far greater than two. All my sensing meters had developed a greater range and depth. The bite of chimichanga and the image of Lauren in front of me were amplified.

She convinced me to drive back because she didn't know the way in the dark. I'd only used a column-mounted shift, and the floor-mounted one took some adjustment, but I had it after a few blocks. The gas pedal summoned more power than I'd ever felt. I wished it made any kind of sense to take the freeway back, but that was out of the way.

At a stoplight, Lauren squeezed my thigh. "You're enjoying this, aren't you? Want to drive around for a while?"

"We should give Terry the takeout while it's still warm."

She laughed. "That's not what's on your mind."

At the house, Lauren gave Terry the enchiladas while I took the stairs to Lauren's room. I didn't have a minute to myself before Lauren came in, kicked off her shoes, and pulled down the covers on her bed.

It wasn't perhaps the right time to ask, but she hadn't mentioned her mom, and I was curious. "What happened to your mom?"

"She got cancer, and it happened very fast. A long time ago. I hardly remember her." She looked away. "Enough talking for now." She moved on top of me, her eyes grazing. "Don't you wish we'd met long ago?"

"I'm not supposed to talk."

She jabbed my shoulder and started wrestling. Wrestling turned to caressing, kissing, embracing, and everything else until we were spent, two nesting spoons asleep, knees up, heads down, and one hand cupping a breast.

***

Next morning, I showered while Lauren packed. When I came back into the room, she'd opened the French doors, and the sun threw flashes off her green earrings. She'd dressed in boots, jeans, a white blouse, and a blue plaid jacket. There wasn't much I could do to help, so I sat in a big chair that looked comfortable but wasn't.

I sensed a sweet and fresh scent. It had been around Lauren before, but it always vanished, just as I noticed it. "What's the aroma?"

"My perfume is one Mom liked. It has violets."

I'd have to study perfumes as part of my new sensory development, but now I listed reasons to be happy. They all had to do with Lauren, and she was leaving. I needed some idle chat to distract me. "Is this a guest room, or is it yours?"

"Guest room. The house was my uncle's, and when he died, my father inherited it. Terry convinced dad to keep it, so she could live here and not in a dorm." Finished packing, she lounged across my lap. "I'm so glad I met you." She hurried a kiss, stood up, and locked her suitcase. Then she sat on the bed, facing me. "Mark!"

Something was coming.

"I want you to see that girl that goes to school with you—the one you told me about. I want you to see her and be nice to her."

I almost stood up. She'd made me feel happy, safe even. And now, so confused. "Are you ditching me?"

"No, no! I just don't know when we're going to see each other again or *if* we will. I don't want to hold on to you if it might not work. But I want to see you again, and I want to write to you."

"I don't understand. I really don't."

"Maybe I don't either, but I don't want you to be lonely."

"I can deal with that."

"But I don't want you to." She sat on my lap again and ran her fingers through my hair. "Promise you'll write to me and that you'll be nice to that girl?"

"I promise I'll write, and I promise I'll think about it." I wanted to know, and I didn't want to ask, but I did anyway. "Will you go out with other guys?"

She frowned. "At that school? Fat chance, but it's for me to decide. I get to choose what I want and be proud, not ashamed."

I shouldn't have asked, but she didn't seem to mind.

She stroked my hair again. "It's time."

I carried her bags to the car and gave a stilted wave as Terry accelerated out of the gravel driveway. I sat on their front steps for a while. Their house reminded me of my grandfather's house: lots of windows and quiet, heavy doors—and all I'd lost with his passing.

Clare

Clare called out to me in the cafeteria, her shoulders open and her hazel eyes welcoming. Her school clothes didn't vary much day-to-day—black turtlenecks and pleated plaid skirts in the cooler months and peasant blouses with lightly colored skirts in warmer months. Her expression was usually serious, but her freckles betrayed a former tomboy. "Right on, Mark! Cool outfit."

I took the seat she'd guarded. "Couldn't decide between my paisley tie and this one, but the stripes seemed to make a more contradictory statement with the work shirt. I only hope the tie isn't a takeoff from some British regiment that massacred Zulus or Boxers."

"Has anyone said anything?"

"No, and I checked the dress code."

She lowered her voice. "I missed you at the SDS meeting Saturday."

Clare and I were the total high school contingent of SDS in Tucson. "Sorry."

She kept to her low, conspiratorial voice. "We have an action tonight. That fascist John Birch Society president is giving a talk to the local chapter. We're going."

"What are we doing?"

"Later," she whispered.

"Can I get a ride?" Lately, I'd been just meeting Clare at these events.

Eyes squinching, she asked, "You want a ride?"

Just loud enough for the entire table to hear, I said, "Yes, I'm asking the loveliest girl in all Tucson for a ride."

A nice blush and smile were interrupted by Dean Gall. "What is the meaning of wearing a tie with a shirt like that?" His upper lip and nose were receding into his cranial vacuum.

"Meaning, sir?" I smiled earnestly as he stood at the end of the table. "The young Republicans over there wear dress shirts and ties, as do you Dean Gall. Those shirts mean conformity. I just have a humble work shirt to go with my tie. That says nonconformity."

If his neck kept expanding, we'd soon see whether his tie was a clip-on or not. "You, young man, are too smart for your own good."

"Would that be like Galileo or Socrates, sir?"

His top button popped, the clip-on tie fell, and he stuttered, "We'll… We'll… Mr. Stenrud." He held himself back from saying anything further and scurried off.

I reached for Clare's hand under the table and whispered, "West exit after the last bell."

***

Clare stood by the exit, a brightly colored Huichol book bag over her shoulder. The taut skin around her eyes and cheekbones gave the illusion that she was close to crying.

I didn't bother asking to carry her bag. She never wanted me to. I'd like to carry it, but she thought that was too traditional and that she should be independent.

"I forgot to ask earlier. Where are your pins?" she asked.

Told her all about it.

"My dad and mom would have helped you get a lawyer."

"I know they would, but I have to do things on my own."

She nodded, and we walked in silence alongside three of the main types of Tucson middle-class front yards: native cacti, imported lawns, and gravel painted green.

After a second quick glance, she said, "I've been missing you. Our talks. Our…"

"Me too." I usually walked anywhere at a fast pace, but I was almost dawdling. We'd been best friends until we'd done it. So awkward with my mind polluted by that Florida bitch. Maybe I was free of that now, and it just slipped out. "Clare, can I kiss you?"

There was no artifice about Clare, and no way to hide glee.

Kiss lingering until she said, "It was messed up last time. I'm sure it was me. I…"

"No. It was me, but can we try again?"

Always a quick thinker, she said, "Mom and dad won't be home for at least two hours." She took my hand and started up the street, but I resisted her pace, and we ambled, giving me time to gather myself.

Today had to work. It had been so easy with Lauren, but Clare and I would be quite sober. Fortunately, Ilona, my Hungarian revolutionary and instructress, had been full of lessons.

Clare's bedroom was a shrine to revolution and free thinkers. Che Guevara had to compete for a place of honor on the wall with Thoreau. But the largest print was Delacroix's *Liberty Leading the People.*

She locked the door and moved between me and her bed. "Tell me what you were thinking."

"I imagined admiring your breasts while you took off your top. I kissed all around your left breast. Then the nipple. Of course, the left first."

She pulled her turtleneck off. "Yes. Start with the left."

I did and lost all sense of time. All sense but Clare at my touch. Clare at my eye. Clare's touch exploring until she urged me.

Joy on her face. Had this really happened? I slid to her side, my eyes never leaving her. She pushed me on my back, covering me with her skin. "This must be what it's really like."

Unfortunately, on top of me, she saw the clock on the bedside table, and her serious look returned. "We have to get ready, and you can't go in that shirt. We have to look conservative." She got out of bed. I didn't, content to watch all of her.

She caught me and blushed. "Hurry up!"

I dressed and waited in the living room, browsing a book on cliff dwellings. She came hurtling down the stairs in a plaid skirt and a navy blouse, carrying a jacket. We drove to my place in her old VW station wagon. Didn't see Mother's car and we parked in front of the trailer.

I ran in, put on a dress shirt, and grabbed my good sport coat. Came out to see Mother standing by the VW in a tight purple blouse, her hair all done up, and talking to Clare through the open driver's window.

"Mother, we've really got to go. We have a meeting."

She gave me a stare. "Didn't I teach you not to interrupt?"

I took my seat and shut the door.

Clare said, "I'm sorry, Mrs. Stenrud. We're late."

"What did she want?" I asked as Clare drove off.

"The loan she asked my parents about."

"Bitch!"

"Don't worry. My folks won't do it."

"Thank God. You know that was the first time she went to a school event of mine."

"At least she went to that one."

"She only went to lay a scheme on someone." I retreated into my shell until I didn't like the silence anymore. "Tell me what's happening tonight, and what I'm supposed to do."

"The head of the John Birch Society, Robert Welch, is speaking at a hotel. The one between the freeway and the art museum. Jeff and Donna are going to ask to present a gift from a local student association. We're just supposed to look nice and respectful and stand along a wall near the exit while Jeff and Donna give the present."

The Birchers deserved some agitprop. They could just as well be the KKK; they just didn't wear sheets. "We're supposed to be ready to run and make sure Jeff and Donna get out?"

"Yes, that's all of it."

She pulled into the parking lot and left the car near an exit, pointed out for a fast getaway. The main entrance reminded me of Javelina High with its curved roof and multiple doors. The crowd in the main lobby moved in one direction. We followed and soon found some of our people looking for stragglers, which were apparently just me and Clare. We moved along the sidewall toward the front of the room until we were just behind our SDS leaders, Jeff and Donna. Clean-shaven, Jeff looked as straight and serious as the Birchers. Donna had ditched her standard black monochrome uniform for a light blue dress. She acknowledged us with a nod.

Clare nudged right up against me, bodies just touching, and after a moment, I wondered if she was having as hard of a time focusing on the stage as I was with only our clothes between us.

There were twenty of us along the wall, and at least two hundred of them were seated or taking their seats. Outnumbered again! Even if we'd included the dead giveaways with long hair or beards, we'd still have been completely outnumbered.

This crowd was deadly alike—all Anglo and genetically incapable of smiling. Their faces had two options: pale or bright pink. They'd all been spawned by Immaculate Conception. How else would it have been possible? I thought of how Darwin's finches adapted to so many environments. These people could vanish with any dramatic shift.

Three old men in suits sat at a table on the stage. One took the podium and addressed the crowd. "You've come to honor our leader, our founder, our president, Robert Welch."

The Bircher congregation stood and applauded. We were already standing and joined in the applause. Slowly, the real audience took their seats.

The speaker went on. "Before we hear from our president, a local student group, dedicated to the ideals of our Republic, has a gift of appreciation for President Welch."

Muted applause as Donna and Jeff tread the carpeted steps to the stage. Jeff took the microphone. "Ladies and gentlemen, President Welch." He turned his body toward the presenter's table. "We, the Students for American Democracy and Entropy, are proud to honor your founder, your president, with a gift symbolic of his many contributions to our Republic."

Thank God he'd made that short. Donna held the gift box on the side of the podium nearest to us as Welch approached her, nodding right and left to his troops. He was rather handsome and smiled warmly at Donna and Jeff.

Clare nudged me, and I saw a classmate of ours in the audience. He saw us, did a double take, and tried to get his father's attention. But the old man just put a finger to his lips and kept his gaze on his president. I guessed there was something to be said for parental control.

Welch accepted the gift graciously from Donna and showed it to the audience—a rectangular box, about three feet by two, wrapped in bright blue paper with a big red ribbon. The first speaker helped hold it as Welch took off the ribbon and removed the wrapping paper without a rip. All eyes were on Welch as Donna and Jeff backed toward the platform stairs.

Welch beamed as he lifted the top off the box. "It's an American flag, and it appears to be properly folded." He held the flag up and out for the audience. Respectful silence turned to gasps as the straps and buckles of an American flag straitjacket came into full view.

Our classmate pointed vigorously at us and now had his dad's attention. As the man got up and tried to make his way to the stage, we left promptly with some of the Birchers following. Our cars were all over the lot, and we scattered to them. Halfway to Clare's car, we noticed two Birchers starting toward us from the hotel entrance. She said, "I'll get the car."

Clare and I had something special. We didn't have to explain everything. I watched her hightail it to the car and took a few fast steps toward the approaching Birchers. It was a trick I'd learned growing up in some exciting neighborhoods. I wouldn't try it with serious thugs, but these two paused for a moment, and that was all I needed. Clare had the car idling by the exit. I hopped in, and we sped off, laughing as we went.

Most of the gang went to the Minus One. There wasn't a band tonight—they were just going for a rehash and celebration—but Clare drove to El Charro over on Broadway. She wanted to eat there, maybe for the last time, before they bulldozed the whole barrio for plunder, urban renewal, and the glory of the white race.

She wanted to practice her Spanish and ordered for the both of us. After the waitress left, Clare asked, "Have you done any thinking about a college major?"

"Engineering with a drama minor or maybe the other way around."

A gentle frown preceded her reply. "You have to be serious about this, so we have options to go to the same school or ones nearby."

"I want to be a renaissance man. What major is that?" She gave me a little kick under the table. First time for anything like that, but I liked it, and it somehow made me feel closer to her. "You decide first. You're more disciplined than me."

"That we know." She sipped her fruit soda and tilted her head as she always did when she didn't have the answer right away. "I've narrowed it to the hard sciences: biology, chemistry, and maybe biochemistry. Math's too boring."

"Those sound right for you."

The food arrived, interrupting our discussion. My taste buds lit up, but then memories of eating Mexican food with Lauren took over. Guilt intruded. But why? Maybe I'd never see her again. But I wanted to.

"What's the matter?" Clare asked.

"Nothing. Just tired." I was saved from having to hide my thoughts and feelings for much longer. Clare was tired too and dropped me off near my place.

***

The rest of the week consisted of boring days at school, afternoons of discovering different tempos and styles in Clare's bed, and a variety of evening entertainments: movies at the Loft, music at the Minus One, or just reading in my room. Friday night, Clare's dad—Professor E.—wanted to talk to me, and I was worried something was wrong. Since Monday afternoon, Clare's heretofore deadly serious expression now shared time with a glowing smile. I couldn't be the only one who remembered Scarlett waking up in *Gone with the Wind.*

But no, all he wanted was to ask if I could watch their house over Thanksgiving. They were leaving next Wednesday and wouldn't be back until late Monday. I agreed, but remembering an invitation to hike and camp overnight, I said it was possible I'd be away myself one night. Prof. E. was fine with that. I just had to tell his neighbors when I'd be gone.

***

Late Saturday morning, there were fifty or sixty of us at a march against the Vietnam War—a few grandparents, a few professors, two babies in strollers, college kids, me, and Clare. Jeff and an older man reminded me that I couldn't react to anyone yelling at us. I protested that I only did that once months ago. They didn't care. They wanted to make sure I remembered. We started out north on Park Avenue, carrying our signs and banners. Once we headed east on Speedway Boulevard, our fair share of abuse commenced—yelling, shouting, screaming, and even spitting at us from cars driving by. We were commies, pinkos, cowards, yellow bellies, and most insulting of all—idiots. Insults hurled from the safety of rapidly moving cars. I expected it from the pickup trucks but not from the young plump mother in a sedan, holding a baby and yelling from a passenger seat.

I kind of liked the us vs. them dynamic. I sure didn't want to be a part of them—the unthinking, the warmongers. Coming to these demonstrations, to our little guerrilla theater actions, I felt like I belonged to something.

When the march was over, Clare introduced me to a retired pediatrician. He'd been her doctor when she was little. His brown eyes twinkled, and just a little gray hair reached out from under his Panama. I told him that his geometric-patterned bow tie looked really cool. He took it off and offered it to me, saying that he didn't have much use for it anymore and that he had so many. I accepted, and he showed me how to tie it on, which took many attempts, driving Clare to unusual laughter. I thanked him profusely, and he hoped to see us at the next march.

Clare and I took a long detour on the way back to her car. We stopped and chatted on a bench, kissed under a tree, and sprawled on a lawn. Bought an ice cream cone and took turns holding it for the other to lick. She plunked my nose with the last of it and took off running. I chased her, slowing every time I got close, until we reached her car.

"Base!" She yelled and faced me, leaning back against the passenger door and breathing deep. Mouth slightly pursed. Chest moving in and out. Eyes as open as could be.

***

Sunday, I had to finish a term paper and do some odd jobs for Mr. Threckel, the proprietor of the Oasis for Mobile Living. A retired Air Force mechanic, he fixed anything mechanical. Most importantly, he kept the water pressure in the showers at optimum force. He paid me to do the menial stuff—weeding the small cactus gardens, maintaining the rock boundaries separating the individual lots, and making sure all the signs were clean. Working for him, along with taking on some irregular moving jobs, were my sources of cash.

Weeding the cactus garden at the entrance, I saw Chas pull up in his Citroën. He handed me a letter and said, "Lauren will be in Scottsdale for Thanksgiving."

I'd expected this, but now it felt strange, and I didn't know what to say.

"I'll be away for the holiday, but feel free to come by my place or Terry's anytime."

I promised to come by, finished the cactus garden, and checked my hours with Threckel. He paid for the last few weeks and went back to his beers, his one-eyed cat, and football on the TV.

My temple of hygiene was empty, as usual, and under the full power of my favorite showerhead, I pondered my future sins, transgressions, or (better yet) quirks. French kings had wives and lovers; Mormons and Muslims had lots of wives. But two girlfriends didn't feel right. Or was that thought just some hangover from too many priests, nuns, and my altar boy goodness?

***

My chemistry teacher, Mr. Boone, was behind his desk Monday morning, his eyes on the far wall. I made a show of adjusting my new bow tie. "Good morning, Mr. Boone. I hope you enjoyed Sunday church service." He ground his teeth. I took my stool in the back and awaited instructions. Finished the experiments and tried to work on some poems. But I couldn't focus. My teenage conscience and pure lust fought pitched battles with chaste images of Clare and Lauren reporting from the front lines.

Clare and Lauren were so different. I started rating them on some half-considered criteria but became revolted with myself when I thought of judges holding up numbers. Wished I had someone to talk with. My few guy friends might boast of conquests but, in reality, hardly had any experience with one girl. Still, what was wrong with having two girlfriends? I wasn't an altar boy anymore. Lauren had wanted me to, or so she'd said. I realized the whole problem was that I didn't want to hurt Clare.

School was over, and there she was at the Linden Street exit. Something was new. She had her hair out of the ponytail, and it fell with a few curls over her ears and to her shoulders. She tilted her gaze up at me, taking me in.

I reached for her book bag, and this time, she relented. "Like your hair down," I said. "I mean, I like it in a ponytail too, but you look different with it down."

She walked. "How do you mean different?"

"The ponytail makes you look more studious and political. With your hair down, you look more intellectual and feminine."

In her bedroom, I brushed her hair back to see the short wafting strands in front of her ears. They always caught my eye when she wore a ponytail. She cut short my admiration of those special hairs by unbuttoning my shirt. But after our frolic, my thoughts about being a two-timing shit came back.

She had something more mundane on her mind. She couldn't see me tomorrow. She had to go gift shopping with her mom and then to a dinner. Wednesday, she was leaving for Thanksgiving in San Diego. We'd be away from each other for a whole week. I didn't know if I could tell her or not, but now it was all put off. I simply couldn't hurt her before she left.

***

Took the bus north Saturday morning. I had thought of hitchhiking, but I'd had bad experiences in the past. So, I paid up and left the driving to a gaunt, tobacco-chewing fellow.

At the station in Phoenix, I wanted to jump off the bus, but everyone in front of me was leaving too and taking their time getting packages and bags off the top rack. Unable to move forward, I looked out the small window and saw Lauren scanning for me. Out of the bus, she gave me a tight hug and a knowing kiss. I started to put my hand through her still short, blond hair, but she stopped me, before changing her mind. "It's okay. You can."

"No. I'll wait till we're alone."

I followed her to the exit, weaving through passengers and rows of sad seating. She pleaded with her eyes as we reached her Pontiac. "When we get near my house, could you lie down in the backseat? I don't want the neighbors to see. They'll tell my dad."

"He's not there?"

"We'll be all alone."

I couldn't believe it. "How'd that happen?" All I got for an explanation was a triumphant smirk.

In her garage, she apologized again, but there was no need. Once inside the house, we stopped in a large living room with a cool, reddish-brown tile floor, covered partly with Navajo rugs, including one with a big white and red biplane. I hadn't seen the outside of the house, but here the walls were burnt adobe brick. I liked the feel of the place—uncluttered, welcoming, and calm.

Lauren stood a few feet away and asked, "Want a soda?"

I'd been dreaming of this moment for days. "No, thanks." I just wanted her.

I watched her eyes wander all over me. Watched her breathe in and out. Felt her hand take mine and lead me down a hall.

***

Much later, we ventured into the kitchen. "I bought a chicken for dinner," she said.

"What are we going to do with it?" My kitchen skills were limited to openers, the toaster, and sandwich making.

"I like chicken breast." She brought a bag out from the refrigerator.

"That's the whole chicken."

"So?" She looked from the bag to me. "Are we going to have our first fight over a bird?"

"I don't know what to do with it. Do you?" I asked, but she didn't.

My brilliant idea was to find cookbooks, but her dad had stashed all her mom's books away after she died. Terry kept a few on a side shelf, but they were all dessert books. I looked at Lauren. She really wanted chicken. Cooking one was an unanticipated test of my manhood, but I recovered and consulted the dessert books, deciding a chicken should be cooked at least as hot as a cherry pie but much longer since it was meat, not fruit. She unwrapped the chicken, fluid spilling out of the bag. We wiped up the mess and put the little chicken in the oven, planning to check it in fifty minutes, the shortest cherry pie time we found.

"Sorry. I don't have any weed," she said.

"That's okay. I don't smoke much. That night on the hill was only my fifth or sixth time."

"We could open some wine. My dad has tons. He won't miss it." A small room off the kitchen was stocked with wine, some in a refrigerated section.

She pulled a slender bottle with a French label from the refrigerated part, opened it, and poured a little in two glasses. "Dad doesn't drink it like he does beer. He sips it."

It tasted somewhat like the smell of flowers and something mineral. Not completely like either but a little of each and something else I couldn't name. We sat in the living room, sipping the wine and eating carrots.

"Why'd your dad put away all your mom's cookbooks?" I asked.

"He really, really loved her, and it made him sad to see them. Terry told me she loved to cook."

"You never had a stepmom or anything like that?"

"No, Terry's the only mom I've ever really had. We have a cook, and she's been here a long time. She likes me, but she's not a mom. I mean— I like her, and we talk. But not about private things." She set her glass down and stretched out on the sofa. Head on my lap, looking up at me. "Tell me, did you see that girl at your school?"

That bugged me. "Why are you calling her *that girl?*"

"You've never told me her name. But you did, didn't you?"

"Yes."

"Tell her about me?"

"No," I said, too loud.

Her eyes widened. "Why not? Are you ashamed of me?"

I shifted on the sofa so fast I jostled her. "I'm not ashamed of you!"

She sat up, rubbing her neck. "You hurt me."

"Sorry. I didn't mean to. I was just surprised when you accused me—"

"I just asked, and I was joking anyway." She reclined back onto my lap. Her breasts readjusting under her T-shirt, removing any desire to argue.

"Is your neck okay?" I asked.

"Yes, and I know you're not ashamed of me."

I started confessing, except there was no screen and no priest. "Her name is Clare."

"And you've been doing it with her?"

I didn't need to answer; she read my face. "You know this is really hard for me."

"Tell me what she's like."

"She's really political, very committed. I am too, but she's more diligent. She'd never miss a meeting, and I skip them sometimes to go to poetry readings or that one time to be with you." I stopped, hoping that was enough.

"Go on."

"Go on where?"

"What color are her eyes?"

"Hazel."

She covered her eyes. "What color are mine?"

"Blue!"

"Terry told me Chas doesn't remember the color of her eyes."

I wondered why he wouldn't and I would when we smelled something burning. Lauren ran for the oven and opened it, unleashing waves of smoke. She closed the door and turned to me with a frown heavily accented by dabs of smoke. It was too funny, and I couldn't help laughing.

Hands firmly on her hips, she said, "It's not funny. I wanted chicken."

"Come on. I have to show you." I turned the oven off, took her hand, and led her to the mirror in her bathroom. Now she couldn't stop laughing. Being a logical guy, I knew the only reasonable thing for us to do was to jump in the shower.

***

Next morning, we cleaned up the kitchen, and she put out placemats, folded napkins, spoons, cereal, and milk. All just so.

"Mark, I didn't tell you one thing."

Put my spoon down.

"I told my shrink. About us." She paused for my reaction, but I'd gone into my numb place. She hurried on. "She has to keep it a secret. That's the law. I told her about you, what you'd gone through, and how you made me feel." She started to cry. "Are you angry with me?"

"No, not angry. Something but not angry."

"You can be angry."

"I don't want to be angry." I was though.

"She's the only one there that I'm comfortable with. She said you sounded like a great young man and that you helped me heal because I finally learned a man could be good to me. But she said I'm not ready for a relationship since I have so much to deal with."

She had more to say but couldn't go on.

I could guess though. "She thinks we should stop?"

"Yes."

"What do you want?"

"I want to get out of there and be free and…" She looked away from me, and I knew what was coming. "I hope later we can find each other…"

I breathed at a pure maintenance level. Tears were trying to form, but I wouldn't let them.

"Mark?" She moved closer and wiped away her tears. "We don't have much more time, and we can be so nice to each other."

I was too numb at first, but it was she who'd brought me out of my shell, and I didn't want to crawl back in it.

***

Lauren had bought a ticket for me to fly with her as far as Tucson. I wanted to take the bus and pay my way, but she and Terry had put a lot of effort into getting the ticket on Thanksgiving weekend, so we could be together for a little longer. On the plane, she held my hand and rested her head on my shoulder, but we didn't talk. After landing in Tucson, we parted awkwardly, but then she ran to the exit door for one

67

long embrace. She only broke apart when a stewardess gently pulled on her shoulder.

In the terminal, I sat raw and numb in the first uncrowded place I could find. Tried to hold onto the image of her running down the aisle toward me, but I lost it. It'd been such a joy to be with her, safe in our own little world—until she burst it.

I went looking for a bus, but the last one had already left. It was a good ten miles to Clare's house or my place—a long walk at night, mostly through a part of town I didn't know. I got Mother on the phone. She said she'd come.

There were hardly any friendly or unfriendly faces inside the terminal, just a harsh light bouncing off hard surfaces and aged aromas of sweat and cleaning products. Outside, there wasn't any wind, not even a breeze to clear out the smell of the airplanes and the parking lot. I couldn't find a comfortable place to sit, so I sat on the ground, leaning my back into a concrete bench.

If Mother left right away, it would take her half an hour to get here. I hated waiting but managed to drift off.

Philadelphia, 1957

Mother didn't look good, and Claude wasn't happy. They didn't tell me where we were going. Claude just said to be quiet. Grandpa took me this way once to the Phillies, but the season was over.

Claude stopped the car and looked at a map. So many cars kept going by; I couldn't read the signs on the market across the street. "It's not far," said Claude and started driving again. After two blocks, he made a left turn.

Mother said, "You passed it."

"Don't want to park right in front." He made some more turns and parked at a corner with my side of the car next to the curb. The red brick buildings were right next to each other, and each one had six or seven steps down to the sidewalk.

Mother looked back at me. The stuff she put around her eyes was leaking down her face. "Claude and I have to visit someone. We won't be long. Don't get out of the car. Something bad will happen if you get out."

Grandpa had told me about places where all the people had dark skin. This place must be one of those. I watched people go by. Some kids came right up to the window and looked in, looked at me. Some smiled. Some stared. Grown-ups took them away. I didn't like being stuck in the car, but I wasn't sure I should disobey and go outside.

There weren't any books or magazines in the back. I crawled over the seat and into the front. In the glove box, there was a book. It had a picture of Claude's car and said, "Your De Soto." Grandpa had already taught me about cars, and the book was boring.

I took out the maps. One was of Delaware. There was Wilmington, and I found New Castle, Dover, and Rehoboth Beach. Then I saw Philadelphia, but it wasn't in Delaware. I saw all the lines on the map. They were roads, but I didn't know which road we were on.

I went back into the rear seat and listened to all the sounds: car noises, people talking, and radios. But I couldn't hear well because I was supposed to keep the windows up. I disobeyed and rolled mine down a little. I could hear a radio. It was different from the radio channels where I lived.

I slept until there was a noise at my window. It was an older lady. I was scared, but she smiled and had a funny sort of hat with different kinds of feathers. I rolled the window down some more and imagined I was a brave soldier in some foreign country.

"Hello, young man."

She wasn't scary.

"My husband saw you at about ten, and it's past two now. You been in the car all this time?"

"Yes, ma'am."

"Where are your folks?"

"I don't know, ma'am."

"Why did they bring you here?"

"I don't know, ma'am."

The lady walked away and talked to a man standing by some steps. They looked back at me. He nodded his head a couple of times. She came back and asked if I needed to use the bathroom.

"Yes, ma'am."

"You can go over to my husband, Mr. Roberts. Over there. He'll take you to our bathroom. I'm going to stay here in case your folks come back." She pointed to the man. "Go on. Hurry now."

Mr. Roberts didn't look mean. He took me up the stairs and into his house. Lace was on all the furniture, and there were framed pictures everywhere. When I was done, Mr. Roberts said he would bring some food out but that I'd better hurry back to the car.

Mrs. Roberts was still there, but she wasn't smiling. Her lips were pushed together. I got in the car, and she said not to worry. She and Mr. Roberts would watch until my folks came. She pointed to her window and said they'd be there. Mr. Roberts gave me something in Reynolds wrap and a bottle of milk.

"Thank you, Mr. and Mrs. Roberts," I said. When they left, I rolled the window most of the way up and pressed the button down on the door. Inside the Reynolds wrap was warm corn bread. I ate it all. Then I drank the milk.

It got dark. No more kids were looking in. I squeezed next to the door to hear a radio playing, but it died out.

Car doors woke me. Mother was in her seat, and Claude started the engine. She didn't say anything. She smelled funny, not like she did when she came home late at night. It was a long drive home.

Last straw

I woke to a rapping sound and a policeman. "You can't sleep here!"

I looked around, scanning the airport entrance drive. "I'm waiting for my ride."

"Where they coming from? You've been here more than an hour."

"More than an hour?"

"Better call them again." He moved off but not far.

I called the trailer from a phone booth near the entrance. Mother answered. "I can't come get you."

"What? You said you would, and the last bus has gone!"

"You should've thought about that before you got on that plane with those drugs."

"What are you talking about Mother? I don't have any drugs!" Remembered there was a cop close by, but I never talked too loudly.

"Ernie says the only reason you'd be flying around is if you were carrying drugs, and he doesn't want any trouble."

"Mother, I don't have any drugs, and I'm out here by myself. Please, come get me."

"I'll think about it. If I'm not there in half an hour, I'm not coming."

I couldn't be pissed off. I had a cop watching me and Mother to deal with. Had to slow the breathing down. Looked for a clock, marked the time, and went back to the bench.

The cop kept up his investigation. "What's the story?"

"Car trouble. Should be here in half an hour."

"Better be. Otherwise, there'll have to be another plan."

I turned on my earnest smile. "Yes, Officer. I can see your dedication to the social order."

He started to say something but stopped short, probably not sure if he'd been complimented.

Half an hour and I'd have to start a long walk. I went back inside and found a free tourist map. Not the best scale but it had the main roads, and I'd have to stick to them until I got to areas I knew. I studied the map and went back outside to wait.

Car headlamps on the entrance road kept turning off before they reached the pickup area. Probably the night shift. A pair of lamps kept coming, and Mother brought the Buick to a screeching halt a few yards past me.

The officer hesitated, probably deciding between a citation and punching out for the night.

"Good night, Officer," I said and opened the passenger door to a waft of tobacco and thirty-dollar perfume.

I got in, and Mother drove off with one of her deep exhales. "You better not have drugs."

"I don't have any drugs."

"You better not."

This stupid accusation was too much. I dumped out my bag—toothbrush, dirty clothes, and everything else—onto my lap. "Look! No drugs!" Took off my jacket, my shirt. "Look! No drugs." Took off my shoes and socks.

"Stop that right now!" she yelled.

Unbelted and unzipped my jeans.

She stopped the car in the middle of the road. "You put your clothes back on, or I'm going to leave you right here."

It was cold, and I put my clothes back on. "I don't have any drugs."

"Why'd you fly then?"

"A girl bought me a ticket."

"You're a gigolo now?"

"What… What's that?"

She was elated. "Mr. High IQ doesn't know something!"

"You can drop me off near the high school."

"Don't you want to know what a gigolo is?"

"I'll look it up."

"It's a man who gets paid to satisfy a woman."

Mother had so many ways of bringing out a calm numbness in me. Under her indirect instruction, I could, at times, reach exquisite levels of self-control. "I'm house-sitting Clare's. Near the high school is good enough."

Silence until she stopped in front of the school. "If you don't start acting respectful, you'll have to find somewhere else to live. Permanent."

"Thanks for the ride." I walked to Clare's, made sure everything was all right, and showered. Went into her room to sleep instead of the guest room. She'd be okay with that, and after a while, memories of her provided some solace.

***

Saturday morning, December 17ᵗʰ. Jeff and Donna's screen door grated and thumped. Obnoxious. Struggled to raise myself from the couch. All the lubricant and smooth contours in my head were gone, replaced by hard-edged things banging into each other. Made it to the door. In came Clare, surrounded by a dress with disturbingly wide red and white stripes.

She surveyed the beer bottles and the main offender, some kind of pink wine. "What happened after I left?"

"Some people came looking for Donna and Jeff. They didn't know they'd gone for the weekend."

She went to sit next to me but stopped. "You need a shower." She picked up empties. "Go ahead. I'll make breakfast."

It was rare, but I could be obedient. The shower didn't help my head, but it might have made me more presentable. She had coffee waiting and put eggs in a pan as I sat down. The coffee was a mistake—I really didn't want to be more aware right now—but the eggs and toast settled my stomach. I wanted to smile at Clare, but oh my God, that dress.

"I don't think I'm going to be a big drinker."

Her stern look changed to inscrutable. "Let's go to Sabino Canyon. You need fresh air."

I wasn't feeling obedient anymore and just wanted to hide under some covers, but guilt intruded, and I went along.

Outside, she started to hand me the keys, thought better of it, and took the wheel herself. That was fine with me. My eyes were uncomfortable just staying open. "Why are you candy striping?" The bold stripes were more distressing than the harsh, low winter sun.

"Mom said I should have some volunteering on my college applications that isn't so purely political." She turned east on River Road. The road dipped, climbed, and curved though small wash after small wash. It wasn't the best for my head, but she was having fun driving, and there was hardly a soul out.

She gained speed down a steep canyon and climbed out fast onto a little plateau, the road littered with sand and little rocks. The VW station wagon couldn't handle the next curve and started skidding. Then, far worse than the skidding, the damn car rolled over onto its side, bumping and banging, hit something hard, and flipped belly up. My hearing stopped, and my vision shifted to slow motion, recording Clare as she thrashed about on her back, feet kicking and hands wild. Then my ears reopened to Clare yelling and yelling, her face horror-stricken.

Heard another car stop. The VW back opened, and two boys our age helped Clare out. I struggled to manipulate my body over and out but couldn't do it until the saviors helped me. Stiff all over. My body hurt in so many places.

Very unlike her, Clare went through a lot of dramatics to convince our Samaritans that we weren't hurt and that we didn't need to go to the hospital. She had them drive us to her house, though she directed them to one that wasn't hers at all. Rather, it was one she was pet sitting for over the holidays.

We got inside, and I sat down, tallying my knocks and bangs. She paced around the living room, still so un-Clare like. I stood up with care and put an arm around her. She didn't look as if anything was broken, and I couldn't see any bleeding. But I asked, "Clare, are you hurt?"

She shook her head, moved away from my arm, and started pacing again.

"Clare, it wasn't your fault. You really weren't going that fast." I wasn't so sure about that, but I hadn't felt danger. "Maybe the tires were old or bald." I wasn't having much effect, but I had to find a way to get through to her, to calm her down.

She stopped pacing and turned on me. "You're so useless. If you weren't hungover, you could've driven. My mom's going to kill me. I left the hospital early, and I wrecked the car for you. *You!*"

Shock. She was in shock. I moved to hold her, to protect her.

"Don't get near me." Ferocious eyes froze me a yard away.

"Clare. Someone will report the car. They'll figure out whose car it is and call your house. You have to call your parents." Finally, she stopped pacing. "Do you want me to call them?" I asked.

"I can call my parents!"

I could usually figure a way out of things, but I had no idea how to help her.

"Look at you just sitting there! You're so fucking useless! Get out! Get out!" She screamed so loud; neighbors would be alarmed.

I felt like a shit. I knew what it was like to be abandoned, but I left because I also knew staying could be even worse.

Even the hot and surging waters of the blockhouse showers at the Oasis for Mobile Living didn't offer much relief. My thoughts roiled. I had no anchor.

***

Tuesday morning with four more shopping days until Christmas. I tried to sleep late, just as I had Sunday and Monday. A knocking on the trailer door woke me. A short man, trying to look imposing in a suit and tie, wanted to talk with me. Said he was the attorney for Professor and Mrs. E.

So what? But I dressed and met him outside. He walked to a big black Cadillac. Amazing. I thought they only made them in black for hearses. I took the front passenger seat. Prof. E. was in the back. He didn't say anything, just stared away from me, content to pay his attorney to hurl accusations and threats.

Shocked that I was being blamed, I went to my numb place and took it. I thought about the whole situation as the lawyer carried on. Could have said I hadn't driven the car. Could have given my own tongue-lashings, but I realized not defending myself would push me toward what I most wanted now—out. Out of this car, out of the trailer, out of Javelina High, out of this town, and far away from Clare.

San Francisco, 1967

There were many ways out of Javelina High—graduation, transfer, death, and just plain quitting. No one remembered anyone actually signing themselves out when dropping, but Grandfather had said I shouldn't walk away from anything I started. So, I strode down Dodge Boulevard to make my last stand. There was no satisfaction in it, though; a clerk gave me a paper to sign and turned her back.

I wanted to go to Berkeley because of the Free Speech Movement, but I didn't know anyone there. I ended up in the Mission District of San Francisco because I knew this guy, Archie, from the poetry readings in Tucson, and he let me crash in his flat. He and his girlfriend had one bedroom, and three single renters had the other three. Walls and floors were bare, except for a few concert posters and some old calendars from neighborhood restaurants and groceries.

The neighborhood used to be mostly Irish, but it was south of the border now, not just Mexico but all of Central America. Seeing so many signs in Spanish made me feel not so far from home.

The post office was hiring, but you had to take a test, and the next one was a week away. Then I'd have to wait for the results. Having to wait was depressing, more depressing was Duane —scrawny, wiry Duane. He claimed the couch in the living room because he'd been there first, which left me with the kitchen floor. He didn't talk much and was angry and threatening if I hung out in the flat during the day, but I dealt with his glare and his threats because I knew that was all he had.

I'd liven up my days by walking three miles up and over the hills to Haight-Ashbury. Young people were all over, and white bread was in the minority. The straights were mostly older Russians, who weren't interested in another revolution, let alone one so colorful.

Haight Street was like the boardwalk in Atlantic City—amusements and diversions at every turn. My first time on the street, I was too awestruck to touch or feel anything, as if it were all behind glass. I surveyed and cataloged everything from Lyon to the start of Golden Gate Park at Stanyan. Thought about checking out the park but couldn't resist walking back along the other side of Haight.

Hipsters, unaffiliated revolutionaries, heads, and freaks leaned on cars, walls, and each other all along the street. I smelled pot every half block and saw smoke a few times but never spotted a joint. Shoppers drifted in and out of delis, boutiques, banks, hardware stores, shoe stores, head shops, and record shops. A whiff of something new started up my stomach. A man stood outside a bakery, eating a small roll that gave off aromas of warm onion, meat, and spice. I went inside, bought a piroshky, and savored every crunchy bite, each little warm taste.

The spell of the street was broken. That little taste had done it, and I walked on, alive and aware. Flyers posted on a telephone pole caught my eye. "Julie, please come home. We love you. Your sister misses you. Call us." Two more like that. One had a lot of white space and I wrote, "Oh, Mother, Mother. Wish I'd another."

Some guy came up to me with a quizzical look. He had long blond hair parted in the middle and a leather strap as a braid across his forehead. Jeans with holes and a dark leather jacket over a T-shirt. He pointed to the pin I had on—*Get out of Vietnam Now*—and said, "That's a downer man." Guy next to him nodded. They walked off. Now I felt out of place, but I left the pin on. For now.

Took me some time to realize the full measure of what dropping out meant. It wasn't just rejecting the values of the straight world. It meant no longer paying attention to the rest of the world. Exceptions were allowed for oriental philosophies and communal theories, but the rest of the world was out. I once visited a Hopi village in northern Arizona. They eked out a living in a traditional way. Saw an old man water his melon plants by carrying a dried gourd to a spring and walking back to each plant. One round trip with that cup-sized gourd for each melon plant. If western civilization disappeared, the Hopis might not notice. We were a long way from that, but we were trying, sort of.

I went into the Print Mint and shuffled around, staying warm and staring at the walls filled with prints and posters of concerts past and concerts to come. Band members stared down at me as if they were the local nobility, laying claim to prerogatives.

Outside, people moved up, down, and across the street like class change at Javelina High. Except here, class change went on all day. Some of the guys looked like they could have walked out of a Tucson poetry reading with khakis or jeans, button-down shirts, and sport coats. Many were more colorful and distinct from the belt up with shirts of all kinds: peasant, pirate, T-shirts with a message, vests with no shirt, and shirts with long, pointed collars. And then there were the jackets and coats: leather with or without fringe, jean jackets, pea coats, cowboy coats, and of course, army surplus jackets.

The girls were far more interesting. Some wore the clothes they'd left from wherever with. Others had arranged some free stuff into a sort of chic. Many had a style free from straightville, even here in damp and cold January. Two stood in front of a tiny tobacco shop at Haight and Masonic. Long unrestrained hair—no, not completely unrestrained. A carved wooden braid above the right ear held the closest one's hair. Strip of flesh between knee-high leather boots and her flower-print dress. Leather jackets, one with fringe on the sleeves, sheltered them from the cold. I knew nothing about them and could barely see their faces, but I was enchanted until they walked off.

***

After a while, I stopped making the trek to the Haight. Hadn't counted on having to wait to take a test and then wait longer for a job offer. Money had run out, and the cold and wind were too strong for my Tucson jacket. One pair of shoes was almost worthless from all the walking I'd done early on, and I had to guard the other pair.

One wrong day, I was alone in the flat with an angry hunger. I went into Archie's room, the furthest room from the top of the stairs. The bed was a box spring and mattress on the floor, nothing else in the room but a chest of drawers. I started to leave but couldn't control the angry hunger. Barely held my hands steady as I went through the drawers and the closet, hoping it wasn't there and begging for it to be there. I found it in a sock—a hundred and thirty-five dollars. I took five and closed the drawer.

I couldn't leave the house. If I didn't spend it, I could put it back. The renters returned to the normal nighttime hustle and bustle. I helped in the kitchen and got a little to eat. The next day though, I was too hungry. I bought a cheeseburger and ate it joylessly. Over the next few days, I used up the rest of the five bucks on hamburgers and bean burritos. Through the week, I was up to a total of eleven bucks from different stashes and was thinking of going to confession but couldn't imagine stepping into a church. They'd have to put the confessional in a library, a post office, or a bus station.

One afternoon, nervous Duane caught up to me walking home from a nearby park. We got to the sidewalk out in front of the building and saw Archie and another renter leaning out the front window. They threw Duane's suitcase out and onto the ground, causing it to burst as it landed. Things fell out. Then out came my pack, hitting the sidewalk hard but staying together.

"Get out of here, you fucking thieves!" Archie yelled.

Duane shouted back. "Fuck you! Fuck you bastards! I better not see you again, or I'll break your face in." He grabbed his case and went east.

I picked up my pack and went inside. I'd stolen, but I had to wait for the mail, my job offer.

Archie stared angrily at me coming up the stairs. "There are more than one hundred dollars missing!"

I gave a legitimate look of disgust. "A hundred dollars! That's a lot."

"You weren't doing this with Duane?"

"No." I was a brazen shit.

They let me off the hook, and I moved to the couch. I didn't take any more money, found a different level of hunger I could live with, and thought about penance.

***

Maybe I didn't ace the postal test, or maybe being a high school dropout didn't help, because all they offered me was a job sorting parcel post on the evening shift at the Rincon Annex by the Embarcadero. Still, I ran to take it and committed myself to contributing from my first paycheck to Archie and the other renters for my stay at their place and for my unacknowledged misdeeds.

First of March, I moved up to the Haight, taking a room in a third floor flat in one of a long line of Edwardians on Fell Street. Our front door was six steps up from the sidewalk, side by side with the doors of the other two flats in the building. Inside our door, a long flight of stairs took a left turn at the top and ended at our central corridor. Every room branched off that corridor: living room, four bedrooms, kitchen, bathroom, and tiny storeroom. I was lucky and moved into a bedroom at the front that had a view of the Panhandle and was furnished with a bed and a chair. I only had to buy sheets and get a little writing desk.

Fell Street was a one-way with three moving traffic lanes and a lane on each side for parallel parking. My room had a view over Fell and onto a park called the Panhandle—ten blocks long, one block wide, and attached to the bottom of the much wider and longer Golden Gate Park. The Panhandle had lots of trees, walking paths, grass, and almost always people—people walking through, sitting, playing, and dancing to bands. It became my front yard, concert hall, playground, and meeting place all rolled into one.

Three others shared the rent. Linda sorted letters at the post office and was my connection to the place. Marie made jewelry and loved guitar players. Jack got a check every month from a trust fund and spent most of every day looking for chicks to ball, which wasn't hard around here. He was dark-haired, good-looking, and tall. Not as tall as I was but tall. He was never satisfied with one girl a day. It had to be at least two and preferably three or more. His room was way in the back, so he could make all the noise he wanted.

I'm sure I didn't see all the chicks he brought in. I slept late and went to work in the afternoon five days a week. I had to miss a lot of them, but I could have cataloged the endless variety of the female form by just photographing his acquaintances. Linda didn't mind, nor did Marie. I didn't either. It drove home to me that half of what held the Haight together was sex. Sex was almost as easy as getting a candy bar—no purchase, just a little flirting and unwrapping.

Other people would stay in our flat now and then. They'd show up knowing one of us or one of the people who lived there before us. If they didn't shack up with somebody, we'd let them stay a day or two in the little storage room, where we had hardly anything to store.

There were faster buses to work, but I liked to walk to the 7 Haight and see the activity in the neighborhood. I'd linger here and there, talking with people I'd met, meeting new ones, and finding out about parties to go to after work or concerts for my days off.

I'd get on the bus at about two in the afternoon and take in the sights as it rolled and lurched down Haight through the Western Addition, turning left on Market toward the Ferry Building. After the first few weeks, I just read along the way, unless a trolley pole came loose from the overhead wires. Then I'd watch the driver get out and perform the reattachment ritual.

The Rincon Annex took up a whole block. Two stories faced Mission Street with a tall first floor and a shorter second. Sculpted dolphins jumped above heavy metal doors set in polished black stone. Eagles, protected in stone barrels, kept a fierce watch on the entrances. Inside, murals telling the history of California ran the length and sides of a long hall. Sharp faces told stories of conflict, violence, hatred, and hope. I liked them all but spent more time looking at the Four Freedoms: of speech, of worship, from want, and from fear. It had a kid reading a great big red book. Citizens came in the front hall to buy stamps at ornate teller windows. None of them ever seemed to look at the murals.

Behind the front hall with its tellers and murals, the real business of the Rincon Annex took place—letter sorting in the middle of the building and parcel sorting in the back. You entered the parcel area halfway down a long corridor and then immediately saw the source of our work at the far end of the room—a ceiling-high chute. Trucks brought parcels, packages, and big flats from all over to be sent out somewhere else in the world or just distributed around the Bay Area. Many of the packages were to and from the GIs in Vietnam.

Unseen to us, the trucks dumped the packages down the chute, and something mechanical kept them from spilling out all at once. Down the chute they came onto a conveyor belt suspended above the main floor. Workers up on a U-shaped walking platform tended the conveyor belt. They'd read an address and toss the package to canvas sided four-foot by four-foot rolling mail carts, which were arranged around the platform by destination. The grunts—me and three others—would exchange empty carts for filled ones and race the filled ones over to the proper truck bay on the left side of the sorting floor. When there was enough to fill a truck, dispatch would call for a truck to back in, and we'd load it, while making sure the carts near the platform never overflowed.

The supervisor of my shift was called The Boss. Big and as black as I'd ever seen, he always wore a dark suit, a white shirt, and a dark hat. If you didn't know him, you might call him fat, but he was as quick as a cat and walked erect, his solid belly leading. He terrified the lazy, the smokers, and any drinkers on the job.

One day, after I'd been there a while, packages stopped flowing down the chute. People and businesses all over the Bay Area had run out of brown wrapping paper. The Boss called us grunts over to the right side of the sorting floor. Every normal day, we'd end up with some packages that nobody could figure out where to send. Maybe the label had fallen off, or it was marked to a state or country nobody had heard of. Or it was written in some script no one could understand. We'd stuff them into big canvas bags and stack them against the right-side wall until a big semitruck came to take them to the undeliverable mail depot in Whynot, North Dakota.

Since, for some reason, no packages were coming down the chute, The Boss had us disassemble the canvas bags on the undeliverable wall, put the packages in rolling carts, and race them to the waiting trucks. The trucks drove off on a discreet circuit, returned, and dumped the packages down the chute. The guys on the platform scattered them among the destination carts, instead of in the undeliverable cart we always kept on the right side. From there on, we mimicked our regular routine of taking filled carts to a truck bay and loading a truck when there was enough to fill it. Except, they didn't drive off to the airport, the Port of Oakland, or some other post office for morning delivery. They just went back to the top of the chute, and the same packages kept going round and round. Seemed a waste to some of the grunts. They were grumbling. But the platform guys and the drivers, who'd been there longer than the grunts, didn't say anything; they just worked. I paid attention to the experienced guys and kept my mouth shut.

A bunch of suits came in to inspect the place. The Boss chatted up the inspectors and toured them around while all the workers kept tending the package merry-go-round. After the inspectors left, The Boss beamed around the floor, smiling, and doing a little jig here and there. He could smell inspectors an hour away.

Due to some unknown set of circumstances, all the platform guys were Filipino. They kept up a running chatter, mostly about the cost of communion dresses, whose wife was on the rag, who was getting any on the side, fishing, and more fishing. They always brought their dinner, and I got to taste pancit and adobo, which were always spicy, bright, and different, depending on whose wife or mother made it.

Sometimes The Boss would get a little shit from the platform but not too much. Something could always go wrong. Packages could stop for no reason just when inspectors were coming, but The Boss knew how to direct the right dramatic scene.

***

I had the day off on Saturday, and in the late morning, I headed out to do my laundry. Tony Patchouli was sitting on the building's steps, hiding behind his dark shades. I doubt I ever knew his eye color. Hair color was easy to remember—black, long, and curly. He was friendly, cautious, and a dealer. He didn't sell to just anybody. You had to know him or be introduced. And even then, he was like the Zam Zam martini man on Haight: if he didn't feel right about you, there was no sale. Most of all, he was cool, which was maybe the most important thing around here. Staying cool was what separated you, and he had his own flying carpet. He was detached on a level plane way above our earthly woes.

It wasn't unusual finding a dealer around here. Without dealers, there wouldn't be any drugs, and drugs were the other half of what held this place together. Sex and drugs. Mind-bending, mind-altering drugs, all the way from sweet Mary Jane to LSD and every psychedelic in between. Yes, we had rock and roll. But there wouldn't be any rock and roll without sex and drugs, at least not the kind of rock and roll they played around here. Almost everybody seemed to deal, at least a little. Anybody needing money for rent could buy a brick of weed or get fronted a brick, break it into lids, make a hundred or a hundred and fifty, and still have weed left over. Or someone would come into town looking to score, and you could do a little brokering. Tony said drug money supported more than half of the Haight.

When I met him, I learned his real name—Pescarola, Pescarino, or something like that. Everyone called him Patchouli, probably because the smell of patchouli was everywhere, and Tony couldn't stand the stuff. Anyhow, I'd forgotten his real name, which was easy to do in this neighborhood. Once he was telling me how he went about dealing, and he described a deal where he'd made a 75 percent profit. I had to point out it was only 66.7 percent. He wasn't upset, just asked me to explain. I did and thereafter became his accounting consultant.

"What's happening, Mark?" he asked as I stood on the steps with my dirty laundry.

"Something, I hope. I have two days off."

"We're dropping tonight. Want to? Two chicks from Berkeley are coming."

How could I say no? "Sure man!"

"We'll get juice and munchies. Got a little bread?"

I gave him seven bucks and headed off with my laundry to the wash and fold.

Tony and two chicks, Charlotte and Renee, rented the second floor flat in my building. We had a sunny day a week or so ago, and I stumbled across Charlotte sunbathing naked in the backyard. She was voluptuous. I should have guessed that, given she always wore a big, loose dress. She looked up from her Lewis Mumford paperback and smiled, pale lips glistening from a bottle of ginger ale. She was on my list of incredibly beautiful and sensual chicks that just didn't turn me on. Something didn't click. She said Mumford believed that humans' perception of time changed centuries ago when bells began tolling the hours in churches in Europe. I took off my watch.

Renee managed to look hip and prim at the same time. Sharp features and cute, though perhaps not pretty. Straight hair in a ponytail. Her shoes always had buckles and went well with her stockings or pantyhose. I had a real thing for her but could never figure out what to say or do. With most chicks, I didn't think about it; I'd just say something. But I always got lost thinking what to say to Renee. I'd smile at her, and she'd smile back, but then she'd walk off or groove with somebody else. She probably got tired waiting for me to say the right thing or anything for that matter.

Tony's flat had a big living room with bay windows that looked onto the Panhandle, two big sofas, and a couple of armchairs. Richard and Mimi Fariña's *Celebrations for a Grey Day* was playing on their KLH 20. The Berkeley chicks, Signe and Anita, smiled back at me from the small sofa, especially Anita with her pigtails and ready look. No place to sit near her, so I took the opposite armchair, and we played eye tag. Her green eyes discovered my hazels, switched to demure, back to inquisitive, and riveted me now and then with expectation.

We were all experienced, and we relaxed—smiling and listening now to Jefferson Airplane as the acid seeped around our brains. It was good stuff, coming on even and smooth. I could see Tony and Renee talking but didn't hear them. Didn't hear the Airplane on the KLH. There was a soft noise with a little jangle, and Renee's arm exuded rainbows and colors. Her arm almost reached me but took the orange juice bottle. Rays from the juice bottle burst all around the room as she shook it, some splattered on me.

My hands were the same size, and the fingers from one hand wove through the gaps between the fingers of the other. Colors darted at me from a spinner as Signe's mouth blew clouds through it. I remembered Anita, and there she was, rotating her neck from side to side on the back of the couch, black pigtails swinging.

The turntable stopped moving. Maybe I should start it again, but the needle moved all by itself. Fucking far out! No, that couldn't be. I got on the floor and crawled to the turntable. The arm was in the holder. It wasn't moving. Turntable was still. Picked it up and lowered it to a groove. White Rabbit!

Crawled back to the chair but stayed on the floor, leaning against the chair. Smiled at Anita. Her smile rode a wave over to me.

Closed my eyes, feeling all right, but I had to piss. Didn't want to move. Didn't but I had to pee. Stood up slow, slow, slower. Smiled at Anita rubbing her neck on the sofa. Went out into the hall. Remembered. Toilet down the hall in its own small room. Opened the door and went in. Tank in front of my eyes, toilet way down there. Shut the door and unbuttoned my jeans. Took out my penis. Hundreds of pricks sprouted from the walls, big ones all the same size, supporting each other and bobbing around. Put my dick back in. They disappeared. God, I had to piss. Pulled it out again and they came back. They got closer to me. I went outside.

Couldn't hold it anymore. Went back in and kept the door open just a little. The walls of penises didn't come back. A long, warm, golden stream colored up the bowl. Cleaned up, shut the door, and sat down in the corridor. Deep breaths. Slow, deep breaths.

Anita came over and sat, her warm leg electric next to mine. Her face came toward me, lips moving. No sound. She pointed at the door. Closed my eyes and swallowed. I stood up, opened the door, and peaked in. Nothing. Whew! I opened it wide. Anita smiled, went in, and closed the door. Triumphant flushing sound filled the corridor. She breezed out and sat next to me, electric legs sparking again. Her face grew older and older and then younger and younger. The words I wanted to say wouldn't come out, but I saw the letters. She put her left hand through my hair, and I purred. Put my arm around her. We kissed, trading tongues.

People came by, used the toilet, and looked at us. We giggled at them, and our voices came back. I pointed. "My room's upstairs."

She nodded, and we went up the back stairs, holding the railing all the way. All was quiet in the flat. Doors shut along the corridor. Giggled all the way down the hall and eased into my bedroom. We became one in my big chair by the bay window. Warm under two blankets, watching cars but mostly the trails connecting our brains to the moving lights. Grew colder and we found my bed. No longer one. I'd become a spider, so many arms and legs all around Anita—the grasshopper—knees up and on her back. Oh lord, this must be heaven. She pulled me and pulled me until my pulsing cannon shot exploding stars, suns, rainbows, and sweet release.

***

I woke up on my back, her flesh all over me.

"My pills! I need my pills."

Connections went off—babies, pills, birth control! "Where are they? I'll get them."

"Leather bag with a red embroidered strap. Think it's behind the sofa upstairs."

"Okay." I threw on yesterday's clothes.

She asked, "Can I shower?"

"Sure, but don't lock it. It's our only bathroom." Then I had a second thought. "If a guy comes in, his name is Jack. Say you're with me."

No one was up in Tony's flat, or at least they weren't making any noise. All the bedroom doors stood shut. I found Anita's bag and returned to shower sounds from the bathroom. I felt like jumping in with her, but it was kind of late to ask. Washed my face in the kitchen sink and went back to my bedroom to dress in clean clothes.

She reappeared and asked, "Can we get some bagels?"

"Bagels?"

"What's the matter?"

"Nothing, just don't know where to get them. We can try up on the street. Couple of bakeries and delis up there."

"But do you like them? Bagels?"

"Seems more like oral exercise than eating."

A momentary frown disappeared into a laugh. "But you'll look for them?"

"Sure."

"Come on then. I'm hungry."

Outside my bedroom, she stopped. "My coat's in the other flat." Down the back stairs, we went again. On the way out, she saw her friend, Signe. They talked while I went outside to bask in the wind and fog.

Anita didn't take long to come out. "Signe's leaving at about one. She's my ride back to Berkeley."

"We've got a couple hours then."

Her interest in bagels lasted only until she saw strudels at the Russian bakery. On the way to the park, I asked, "What are you studying at Cal?"

"Anthropology."

"What part?"

She had a surprised look and held the strudel for a moment. "You know there are parts?"

"You think I'm a dumb hippy?"

An offended look. "No!"

"Just teasing. Your friend, Charlotte, lent me an anthro text."

She answered the question. "Physical anthro. I want to specialize in human evolution."

"Has he?"

Thankfully, she'd finished the strudel because that earned me a two-handed push and a smirk. "Good question."

We walked into the park, heading for Hippy Hill. Most everybody hung out on the grassy slope just below a line of trees. For some reason, the sun was often out, or at least partially out, on that slope, and grass actually grew there. We sat with people I knew and shared some joints.

A sharp voice cut in. "What are you doing here?"

I looked up at the voice and was shocked to see the former Javelina High Homecoming King and Queen looking down at me. Their faces were tighter than the creases on their clothes. The King asked again, "What are you doing here?"

It was a rather stupid question, but I answered, "I live here."

The King's tight mouth turned into a dumb grin. "Figures."

A chick with a smile to wake you up and long, glorious blond hair reflecting the filtered sun held up a joint to the Queen. "This weed's so good. It lights my body all up."

If one of the cats had said something like that, the Homecoming King would have hit him, but his face just grew red. The Queen hesitated with the joint before her, perplexed and curious. The King grabbed the joint, threw it away, and retreated with his queen, to our collective relief.

"I went to high school with them. They were uptight even back then."

A lengthy discussion ensued; the unanimous conclusion being that the Queen wouldn't be straight for long.

Anita and I walked to Signe's car. She gave me her number and said she wanted to see me again but didn't suggest anything specific. I promised to call but lost the number.

Back inside my flat, I found a letter from Lauren in yesterday's mail. The only mail I really wanted these last months was one from Lauren saying she wanted to see me. Or one from Clare saying how sorry she was. I stretched out on my bed and read.

It hit me in the stomach. Don't know why it hit me so hard. Hadn't I given up on her? I needed a long shower and started down the hall, only to see Marie, her back to me, going into the bathroom with her shower stuff. Damn! Went back to my room, rolled two joints, and went searching for the chick with glorious blond hair or maybe one with a different hair color.

***

Days later, I was leaving for work when Tony stopped me on the outside steps, hands uneasy by his hips. "Mark, I need your help."

I'd never seen him anxious before. "Sure man, but I have to go to work."

"No, man. It's now. I'll make it up to you. You never miss work. You can be late once."

He'd lost his cool. I didn't know what it was about. But he was my best friend, so I followed him into his room where two nervous-eyed cats named Mikey and Dennis sat on the edge of the bed. About thirty of the largest bricks of weed I'd ever seen rested in a pile by the closet.

Dennis started talking. "All right, your friend's here. It's time to do the deal." He tried to talk tough, but he didn't look it—skinny, gold-rimmed glasses, and an embroidered vest over a frayed T-shirt.

Mikey, with his slow eyes and thick fingers, looked like he'd be dangerous if you got between him and food when he had the munchies.

"Just hold on." Tony handed me a half-unwrapped brick. "Check it out."

It had a lot more stems than a normal kilo. Hell, they were practically branches. With all that wood, they probably couldn't compress it to the size of a normal brick. I wished he'd told me about all of this before bringing me in here.

"I told Dennis I'd buy thirty kilos." Tony's hands weren't hovering anymore; he jammed them against his hips. "But he brought these bricks packed with fucking stems."

Dennis seemed to think about standing but just said, "I told you they were only forty bucks a piece."

"You didn't tell me they had all these fucking stems."

"What did you want me to do? Talk on the phone about how big they were?"

Someone had to cool this down, so I asked Tony, "How's the weed?"

Dennis said, "It's pretty damn good."

Tony relaxed his hands. "It's not bad."

"Can I try?" I asked.

Dennis gave me some Zig-Zags, and I rolled a joint. A touch rough on the throat but it had a kick with just one toke, and that was enough for now with all this business in front of me. The blue cellophane wrapping on the keys shimmered, and the whole damn pile looked scary. I passed the joint to Tony and he to Dennis, and we left it with Mikey, who probably wouldn't be of any other use.

I was Tony's accounting consultant, so I asked, "How many lids in one of these?"

Tony said, "I wasn't going to sell lids, man. I was going to sell one or two bricks at a time."

"But the weed is good," I said. "If you want to figure out a fair price, we should see how many lids are in these bricks."

Dennis wasn't a help either. "Forty bucks is a good price. We don't need to break one up."

Hell with convincing them. I just started breaking up the unwrapped brick and said, "Get me some baggies."

Mikey saw a chore he liked, moved onto the floor, and helped. Tony found the baggies, and we all went to work. They bitched about the size of some lids, but I kept my mouth shut, adjusted any that looked wrong, and kept the filled ones by my side. We finished with seventeen, but I wasn't sure how many one usually got out of a normal kilo.

"How many do you normally get?"

They weren't going to agree on anything. Tony said twenty-eight, and Dennis said only twenty-four. This was going nowhere, but seventeen was roughly two-thirds of what they'd normally get, so I rounded and said eight hundred dollars should be fair.

Dennis stood. "Fuck. I can't make anything on that." He went to the window, turning his back.

I looked at Tony. "What were you going to sell them for?"

"Sixty-five, seventy." He got off the floor and sat in his chair.

"If you can sell these for forty or forty-five, you should be okay," I said.

"Maybe. They're bigger, riskier to lug around, and more work to break up. And some might have more stems."

Dennis defended his bricks. "And maybe some have more buds! If I sell these to you for eight hundred dollars, I'm hardly making anything. Make it eight hundred and fifty dollars."

Tony said eight hundred and ten dollars, and they agreed on eight hundred and thirty dollars. Tony paid, and Dennis and Mikey left, heading back up the coast.

"Thanks, man. I didn't know what you were doing at first, but you got it worked out." Tony handed me a couple of lids. "I owe you more than that, but I have to get moving. I don't want to sit on all these bricks."

I thought about asking if he needed help, but I wasn't sure I wanted any of this business. "You don't owe me anymore. I have to go though. I can still get to work before I'm too late."

He handed me a five. "Here's for a cab, but you better change your clothes and wash up."

I ran back upstairs, stashed the lids, and changed. Flagged a cab a few blocks away and caught heat from The Boss but not a lot. Work was mindless as usual—shuttling carts and packages around. My thoughts were on a Rudyard Kipling poem about not losing your head. The one and only debt I owed Mother for putting me in so many difficult situations— I could stay calm when trouble arrived.

Death of the Hippy

A Friday morning somewhere in October, and Tony was pulling on my warm covers. "Wake up. Something's going down."

So much partying to wake up from but I turned on my side, still under the covers, and looked up at his grin, bushy black hair, and sunglasses. "Where's…?"

He laughed. "She went to the bathroom. Shower, maybe."

"What are you getting us up for?"

"There's a funeral and procession for the hippy."

"Some hippy's that important?"

"No dumbshit. It's an event—*The Death of the Hippy*."

"You go to too many funerals." He had such a big family that somebody was always dying: an uncle, great-grandmother, somebody. All Tony's sins were forgiven, at least for that day, and they all went to the funeral and a big Italian meal after.

"You go to anti-war protests, and this is a protest against how TV talks about us."

I pulled on a sweater and sat up. He really wanted company, but I wanted to go back to sleep. "Look man, if you really need me, I'm here, but this is baloney. What's the point of dropping out if we care what they think about us?"

He left, but I couldn't go back to sleep. I wasn't political anymore like Tony thought I was. I had the same beliefs, but

I wasn't engaged. Going to a few marches didn't mean much. I'd dropped out and was part of this collection of people who thought they were capturing the perfect world with psychedelics and free love. This was my community now: people who believed for a few moments—a day, a week, a month, a season—that we were onto something lasting, something sacred with this strange brew. And I thought that too, now and then.

***

Early Saturday afternoon, I had breakfast on Haight in a converted pharmacy called the Drogstore Café. They'd wanted to call it the Drugstore Café, but the city wouldn't let them. I sat at the counter, eating eggs and hash browns and staring at the old, wooden pharmacy cabinets. I wondered what it would be like to be a pharmacist. The post office was getting boring, but I wasn't ready for big decisions and finished my breakfast instead.

I walked out the door, only to see two cops projecting the law onto three backward-leaning cats I hadn't seen before. They weren't spiffy, and two looked a little edgy. One of the cops looked me up and down and said, "You. Maybe you know?"

"What can I do for you, Officer?"

"These boys haven't been any help. We want to know why you have so many words for the police. Pigs. Man. Heat."

"Each word means something different, officers." What an opportunity to show off my unrealized professorial skills. "We use *the man* for the whole establishment from LBJ down to a police rookie. But it has to be *the man* with a *the* because we use just plain *man* for ourselves." I looked at the calmest of the three cats. "Hey man, I'm talking to the man right here."

With my audience paying attention, I kept going.

"*Fuzz* is for an officer who's doing something nice. Say one of you two helped that old Russian lady over there to cross the street. Then I'd say, 'Hey man, look at the fuzz helping the old babushka cross the street.' *Heat* is for when you're enforcing the law. Say some straight tries to swipe the babushka's purse. If you run and catch him, I'd say, 'Look man, the heat just popped that dirtbag ripping off the babushka's purse.'"

I took a breath. "Now *pigs* is a special case, Officer. Let's say the head of Safeway calls the mayor and says we need you to do something about the farm workers picketing at our stores. The police go to that Safeway on Stanyan, get all violent, and bang the grape pickers all up with their nightsticks. That would be the *pigs*. Though I'm sure that would never apply to you two officers." I wasn't sure at all, actually.

"Will you look at this, Krumke? We found a smart hippy."

Krumke stopped writing in his notebook. "Smart ass, more like it. What do we call you—hippy, beatnik, head, or just plain goofball?"

"What about me?" I smiled with pride. "I would be a freak, sir, because even if I were straight, I wouldn't be normal."

The fuzz laughed at that. "What do you do for a living, freak?"

"Just like you officers, I'm a public servant, toiling five days a week at the US Postal Service."

Krumke's partner thought he had me. "Then you're part of the man."

Maybe I could finally get into the world famous Zam Zam martini bar. "You see, we're on the same side. Maybe we could share some of those martinis from the Zam Zam man."

No way they'd share martinis with a freak. Krumke took his time looking us up and down. "Just keep your noses clean." They continued their patrol up the Haight-Ashbury delta.

The three cats said, "That was cool, man!" and "Didn't know that's what those words meant."

I said I'd just made it up, which was sort of true, and tried to leave.

The shortest one had a gap in his teeth. "Got some black beauties and a good price for you."

No wonder they were edgy—fucking speed freaks! "Sorry man, I have to split." Speed freaks and junkies were ruining this place.

I beat it toward the Panhandle, that land of psychedelic opportunity. People were passing a joint, and I stopped to help. Across the park, Tony and Renee were talking on the sidewalk in front of our building. I wanted to catch up to Renee, but as I started to head over, she walked off by herself in the other direction. Damn. Running and following just wouldn't be cool.

By the time I reached our building, someone else was talking to Tony. The guy had a big mop of curly brown hair and a black leather jacket over a frilly white shirt. I knew him but couldn't remember his name. They kept talking as I sat on the steps.

The cat walked over to me. "Hey, Mark. I'm Ray. Remember me?" He sat on the same step, angled toward me.

"You had a party with that absurdly good hash, and the chicks did body paint."

"Yeah, that was something." He put a hand on my knee. "I could use a cool head tonight. Tony says you'd be good."

Tony stood in front of us. "I'd do it, Mark. But I have to go to Petaluma tonight."

I was curious and was looking for something different. "What do you need?"

"We're having a cap party. A friend has some acid. He'll bring it buffered, but he needs people to fill the caps. I'll give you some for helping out."

"You've done this before?"

"Once. We'll use the big room at my flat. Most of the people who're in on it are from there. Nobody will bother us."

"Okay. I'm in!"

Ray said, "Good. Come by before seven." He started to leave but stopped and pointed down the street. "Isn't that Jorma from the Airplane getting out of that funny car?"

Tony said, "No, that's Kantner."

I knew the car. "It ain't Grace Slick, but the car's a Citroën. Friend had one."

Ray studied the foreign job and turned to go. "Later, man."

I looked at Tony. "Is this all okay?"

He sat next to me. "Fuck man. I wouldn't set you up for anything wrong. Ray's cool. Sometimes he spaces out, but he's cool. I was going to do it, but my little brother needs me for something."

Later that day, I went up on the street for dinner to the fish and chips place. They served it in a folded newspaper. I splattered malt vinegar all over mine and stood outside, eating and watching the endless parade.

Wasn't sure of the time and waited for somebody to walk by wearing a watch. It took a while to see one, but I asked the time and had to hustle to Ray's.

He answered the doorbell and took me up the stairs and into a dining room. Clean butcher paper covered a large wooden table. Arranged around the table were small scoops, bags of empty capsules, sheets of thick 8.5 x 11 paper, and table knives. Maybe they were butter knives.

One chick had a cold. She couldn't cough around the powder, so there were only seven of us. Ray did a dry run, showing how he wanted us to work—scooping flour on a sheet of paper, using a knife to keep it in a close pile, tamping the capsule parts down into the powder, and pushing the small ends onto the bigger ones.

The doorbell rang, and Ray asked me to go down with him. Guy wasn't from the Haight—good-looking with short blond hair, a straight nose, horn rimmed glasses, turtleneck, blue sport coat, and totally, totally undercover—loafers with tassels.

He sized me up, stayed relaxed, and handed Ray a paper bag. "See you at eight tomorrow morning. Okay, Ray?"

Ray nodded, and the guy left without telling me his name. I wondered why Ray had me come down with him. I was too excited to care about it though. Back upstairs, I took a seat at one end of the table. A pudgy cat with long black hair sat across from me, and a girl sat next to me, smiling under brown bangs.

Ray held out a clear bag with the buffered LSD powder to smiles and nods. We went to work with Ray walking around, watching and helping. He held up sodas for us to drink, poured more powder when needed, gathered up the filled caps, and counted them into bags of one hundred. I was my normal, careful self, keeping the powder to a few fingers and shaking them off now and then. Someone asked for music, and Ray put on some Joan Baez. Not the right time for serious rock. I stood up from the table and stretched my back, which was getting creaky from hunching over. I made more in a shift at the post office, and that didn't hurt my back, but this was exciting.

As I sat back down, I saw a guy across the table lick the powder off his fingers, which wasn't the smartest thing to do until we were done. Watching him reminded me to be careful, and I focused on what was in front of me—the powder, the tools, and the caps. I couldn't miss the cat at the other end banging the table when he stood up.

Ray talked with him, and they went into the living room. Ray came back alone, closing the sliding doors that separated off the living room. He whispered in my ear, "Man, I blew it. I forgot these." He held out a box of disposable gloves in a nervous hand.

That would have been a good idea. People had become clumsy, and I'd even seen a freak in the middle of the table break a cap as he slid the halves together, but instead of tossing it, he swallowed it. I looked at the girl next to me and spoke softly to her. She turned to me with a glorious smile and completely dilated eyes. I turned back to Ray and said, "We better get everyone away from the table."

I helped Ray get people into the living room. But he never came back to the table. I still wasn't feeling any effect, and all I knew was that I didn't want to be the one who made a mess of this. Washed my hands, put on gloves, gathered the powder that was out of the bag, and made some more caps. My neck ached, and I stopped to think. I doubted I'd taken in enough for it to completely come on, but even so, I was sure I couldn't cap all the remaining powder. I closed up shop and counted the caps that had been left out and the ones I'd finished. Checked out the bags Ray had counted. We were short by a little more than three hundred. I straightened up as best as I could and stowed the caps and leftover powder—maybe it was enough for three hundred.

I wanted to join everyone else, but I still wasn't tripping. Just had a little buzz going. Damn, so careful that I hadn't gotten enough. Went and checked out the living room. Two couples were entangled, and the other two were lying close to each other. I was a quarter stoned and, with the chick who was sick not here, the odd man out. I could drop a cap, but I'd still be alone. Instead, I took some wine from the kitchen and sat by a window, sipping it and getting cold. Found a blanket and sort of dozed, watching the rooftops across the street.

Doorbell woke me. I hurried down and let the guy with loafers in, but now he had leather boots. He'd expected Ray but waited on the inside landing while I retrieved his stuff and hurried back. "Everyone else got stoned before we finished. I only got a little buzz and cleaned up."

"Ray get stoned too?"

I nodded. "We didn't remember the gloves."

"Did you know about that before?"

"No."

"I'm Julian. What's your name?"

"Mark."

"Why didn't you get stoned?"

"Careful, I guess. Just a little buzz."

"Why didn't you drop after you cleaned up?"

I explained as his eyes took me in.

"How many caps are filled?"

"We're short by about three hundred. I saved as much powder as I could, maybe enough for the three hundred."

"How would you move three hundred caps?"

That wasn't a hard question. "A friend's a dealer. We could go to the people he buys from."

"Nothing on the street?"

"My friend doesn't. I wouldn't."

"Why don't you cap the rest of the powder and move it for around two bucks a cap in lots of fifty or more. Can you do that?"

"Sure."

"Good. Meet me in Berkeley on Tuesday. There's a coffee house on Euclid, just north of campus. See you at ten. Just you." He offered his hand, and we shook. "I'll talk with Ray later, just let him know you took care of this business."

Back upstairs, everyone was asleep. I left a note for Ray and went home to crash.

***

I found Tony Sunday afternoon and told him everything but Julian's name. We worked together making the caps and sold everything by late Sunday evening. Tuesday, I borrowed a car and drove down Oak Street past all the hitchhikers, onto the freeway, and over the Bay Bridge. I'd studied the map and parked a few blocks from Euclid. I walked into an almost empty coffee house ten minutes early. Ordered a tea and a pastry and took a table by the window. Yesterday's papers were lying around, and I busied myself with *The Chronicle*. There had been a big anti-war march in Washington, and Allen Ginsberg had tried to levitate the Pentagon with chants. It hadn't worked. Damn. If there'd been a big march in DC, I must have missed one here. Well, I'd been busy on Sunday.

Minutes later, Julian sat down with a cup of coffee. "Any problems finding this place?"

"No, studied the map."

He nodded. "Any problems with the other?"

"All done."

"Good. Let's finish our drinks and take a walk." We went up Euclid, past a theater and into a residential district. "I want you to keep the money. Maybe we can work together."

I expected something like this but not that I'd be keeping all of it. "It seems like a lot for what I did."

"Don't worry about it." He offered me hard candy from a round tin with pictures of raspberries embossed on the lid. I liked it—fruity, barely sweet, and soothing. "Tell me about yourself."

I gave him a short version. He asked if I'd ever been busted, and I said, "No."

We started walking back, turned on La Conte, and went into a light blue, three-story building, where he shared an apartment with his partner in psychedelic chemistry. I took an overstuffed chair in his living room. He sat across from me at a low table and removed his horn rims, uncovering cool, blue eyes. "We need people to help us move large quantities of acid."

I nodded, and he went on.

"We're going to turn out batches about every ten days to two weeks. We'd need you to start with five hundred and then move up to a thousand and more. Should I keep talking?"

Excitement was gaining ground on any fear I had. I nodded.

"By the way, we'll have a tablet machine soon, so there won't be any more cap parties." He paused. "Tell me about your dealer friend, the one you off-loaded the caps with."

I told him all about Tony, especially how careful he was.

"It's good to have someone to work with. I have a partner. You'll meet him, but let's keep it at you—and you alone—coming here. Tell Tony we want it that way. Nothing against him."

Hell, I hadn't thought I'd be the main contact. Heavy!

"We like the way you handled the fuckup the other night, but you're inexperienced, and that makes us nervous." He leaned back into his chair but kept his eyes all over me. "Rule number one is—don't get caught. What's that mean to you?"

I was back in school but with more interesting questions. Gave him my thoughts about selling to trusted people, keeping a low profile, and avoiding getting busted for other things like speeding. He talked about keeping up with gossip and news about people around you. He spoke about getting buyers ready before a batch came out, so we'd limit how long we were holding. If we weren't holding, we were pretty safe.

We talked for almost two hours. He gave pointers and asked me questions, going over stuff we'd already gone over. The more we talked, the more he relaxed. Finally, he told me how to keep in touch, when to meet again, and to get ready to move a load of tablets.

I had to ask. "What about Owsley?"

"He has his own lab. He's great for the psychedelic movement, but he is way too out there for us. Like I said, we stay behind the scenes and need you to do the same. Watch what he does, and don't do it."

He opened the door for me, and I left.

Phoenix

Tony and I became rather accomplished in our business with the Berkeley chemists. We weren't greedy and kept four to five mid-level dealers content. Most suppliers sat in their place, waiting for people to come to them. We didn't want inventory, took Mao's advice, and swam with the fishes, just a couple of psychedelic revolutionaries making our deliveries during the day when lots of people were out and about.

Some days, we'd do the whole route together. Today, we split up and went out separately. My last stop was Blake. His building was like mine, three flats served by three front doors, six steps up from the sidewalk. A cat and a chick sat on the bottom step, smelling of weed and honeysuckle, strewing sunflower shells, and drinking chocolate milk out of a carton. I pushed the buzzer and waited. There was a song going around by Howlin' Wolf – "Built for Comfort." It sort of summarized Blake, because he sure wasn't built for speed.

An old lady in a brown coat and black socks came up the steps with groceries.

"Can I help with that, ma'am?"

She looked me over and thought about it. She looked at the two on the bottom step and back at me. My clothes were clean, and my hair was only an inch over my ears, but that was enough, and she shook her head. She put down the groceries to unlock the door.

"Can I hold the door?" I asked.

She nodded, picked up her groceries, got inside, and flashed a quarter smile.

Blake opened his door. "Sorry man. I was on the phone."

Followed his steps one by one up the stairs. "Anyone else here?"

"Just my old lady, but she's asleep."

I sat in the kitchen while he got the money. Calling her his old lady was odd. I mean, she *was*, but I knew both of them. Maybe they were going to split. None of my business. I looked around the kitchen—a few dishes in the sink, counters clean, and even a clean-looking dish towel on a hook.

He came back with cash, and I pushed the tight bag of two hundred and fifty across the table.

"Light blue tabs. That's cool." He twirled his droopy mustache. "You remember Ben? Tall as you but blond hair?"

"Yeah, not a cat the chicks would take to. Sort of sour looking."

"That's him. Cat turned yellow, almost orange. Free clinic sent him to this place downtown."

"You mean that VD clinic?"

"No, that's south of Market. This one's in a building across from city hall."

"So, it's not VD?"

"Something else. You catch it from dirty dishes or bad food. Anyway, they told him to rest and that it would go away. And get this—the cat has to eat liver. Cow's liver."

My new vocation had put an end to boredom. Every day was different. Excitement, thrills, and a few scares along the way, but adventure was always around the corner. The thought of liver, though, temporarily dampened my enthusiasm for any activity. I went home to find an unwelcome envelope delivered by my former employer, the all too reliable US Postal Service. Inside was a smaller envelope from the Selective Service. Mother had scrawled on the back of it—

It's about time you were taught some respect.

The letter demanded my presence at a draft physical in Phoenix and a chance to go to Việt Nam. Heavy! Seriously heavy! I had no chance as a conscientious objector, since I had no history of it. Besides, I didn't think all wars were wrong. This one was though, and resisting the draft was going to require a new level of commitment. More than marching, more than wearing pins.

I went over to the bowling alley on Haight to catch the gossip and get some advice. Guy at the cash register recognized me when I asked for size twelves. "Do you ever actually bowl?"

"Not exactly. I cheer on the other cats."

"Sure don't look like a cheerleader." He placed the bowling shoes on the counter with an exceptionally nuanced smirk.

They were at the last two lanes. I found a seat and listened to the local news. Stewie MacFarlane had gotten popped with a kilo of weed. He was a worthless fuck, full of rumors, and always shorting people. He was out on bail, and the word was to watch out for him; he'd do anything to stay out of jail. Jed had been half a hero. He saw some chick getting ripped off on Haight across from Buena Vista Park. He ran after the prick and almost caught up with him, but the robber turned on him with a knife. Nothing he could do then. Not much other news, so I gave mine.

"You're screwed, man!" I didn't know who said it, but the conclusion was unanimous. "You may as well kiss your ass goodbye as soon as you set foot in that place in Oakland."

"Mine's not in Oakland. Mine's in Phoenix."

Karl, one of the oldest bowlers, said, "You caught a break, Stenrud." He was at least twenty-three and always wore a railroad cap over his steel wire rims. "People used to get 4Fs by just acting weird in Oakland, but the draft board got wise to it, and they'll slap a 1A on you and off to Vietnam you go. Phoenix though, you might have a chance."

I had a long chat with Karl about the general scarcity of freaks in Arizona and what might constitute 4F behavior to an Arizona draft board. We decided I'd have to act permanently weird for the physical, not over the top by putting on a show. Just believably, permanently weird. We figured if I was on the tail end of a trip, I'd have that what's-going-on-around-me stoner look, but I needed control, so acid was out.

Needing something mellow, I bought two psilocybin caps from a friend and vitamin capsules from the local drug store. Back at my flat, I emptied eight of the vitamin caps and the two psilocybin caps into two separate piles. Tossed enough vitamin powder to make room for the psilocybin, mixed the two piles thoroughly, and filled eight capsules, which I put by themselves in the vitamin bottle.

I organized my clothes for the trip: khakis and a corduroy jacket for the plane and jeans, the olive work shirt Lauren bought me, and a paisley tie for the physical. Looked at my neatly arranged shoes in the closet for a long time and picked out some sneakers and desert boots.

On the plane, there were two nice-looking straight chicks with almost identical hair—lifting off the top of the skull, looping down the sides and back of the head, and ending in a big curl that flipped up at chin level. No sign of ears. Their hair must have taken hours to get into that arranged rigidity. I liked almost any hairstyle on a girl as long as it wasn't chemically preserved. I particularly liked a few little stray hairs wafting independently around the ears. It gave me something extra to notice and charge up my senses.

I paid for two nights at a motel near the airport, and the desk agent gave me a room on the top floor, far from any other occupied one. All the rooms opened onto an outside corridor. Mine had a big bed and a TV. Shower was in the bath, but the water pressure was acceptable. Checked out the vending machines and settled for three cans of ginger ale. They'd go well with my supplies—bananas, sesame butter, and graham crackers.

I did my calculations: 0830 for the physical, 0800 for the taxi, drop caps at 0100.

The radio had been censored by a committee comprising the Pope, George Wallace, and Liberace. *Star Trek* wasn't on tonight, and nothing else on the TV interested me. I pulled out the Phoenix phone book and thought about Lauren. I could call, but she had another guy. Didn't want to think about it anymore, so I used a spoon to stir up the sesame butter and make gooey swirls on my crackers.

Near midnight, I patrolled the room, looking for sharp edges and corners. The TV table was near the end of the bed, so I wrestled the TV to the ground and moved the table into the bathtub. Then, with extra pillows and blankets from the closet, I built up a protected place in the corner beside the bed. I opened the windows and looked outside. Quiet. Sky Harbor had shut down for the night, but I couldn't and dropped one full dose at 0100. Sillysybin! Sweet Sillysybin! Stretched out on the bed and searched for a soft song to sing to myself. "I Shall Be Released" maybe. Then I found it. Peter, Paul and Mary, mostly Mary—"Leaving on a Jet Plane."

The folds of the burgundy window curtains billowed and flapped. They'd approach the bed, retreat, and then return. Hilarious! They were trying to flirt with me. I felt a big smile inside and stretched out closer to the curtains, but they wouldn't tickle. Stood up among their enveloping ripples, letting them caress me. Thought of sails and *Horatio Hornblower*. Too much violence. *Moby Dick*. Oh no, the whale. *Old Man and the Sea*. All those sharks.

Got back to my corner and let the images flow away from the sea and the sails. Peeled a banana and chuckled. Laughed and laughed until I floated in a warm yellow and a soft blue…

***

BUZZ! BUZZ! BUZZ! The alarm pulled me into the world. Remembered where I was and looked at the still curtains. I banged a few walls but put the TV table back in place and the TV back on top. Dang. Table was backward. TV was right though. Couldn't worry about that, just flushed the remaining evidence. One dose had been enough. I confronted the mirror. My hair was all over the place, and I looked like crap.

Made sure the Do Not Disturb sign hung on the door and walked to the lobby. Taxi was waiting and dropped me off at my destination with five minutes to spare. I thought it'd be in some military building. But no, it was just a big office building. Out front, all sorts of people stood around in groups, waiting for their appointments with the imperial recruiter. Blacks, Mexican Americans, Anglos, but hardly any Brooks Brothers. No obvious freaks.

None of them wanted to be there. Had they wanted to be heroes, they could've enlisted. No, none of them wanted to be there, but they wouldn't admit it, wouldn't admit they were afraid. The worst pranced around harassing the smaller ones, showing the world that if they could bully a hundred-and-twenty-pound clerk, they could take on the toughest Việt Cong. They eyed me, didn't know what to think, and left me alone, other than an occasional stare. I wondered if my resistance came from something more than believing it was an unjust war. As best I could tell in my receding psilocybin haze, I wasn't afraid of dying. No, that didn't bother me, but I didn't know if I could handle being mangled or crippled.

The doors opened, and a man in a uniform hurried us into a large room with seventy or so of those high school desks with the movable writing arms. He called roll and had us sit in alphabetical order. My mind was clearing. There were only a few glittering trails if I turned my head too fast.

At the front of the room, another man in a uniform wore an odd-looking hat with a flat brim and a creased crown. He gave instructions while the uniform without a hat passed around booklets, answer sheets, and pencils. Damn. An IQ test. Did Karl tell me about this? They told us to start the verbal section. I glanced at a few pages and came up with a strategy—UA for unclear or ambiguous, FC for false choice, and TMA for two or more acceptable answers. Any question I couldn't find a problem with, I'd answer. Finished the verbal part and closed my eyes. Raced through the math section. No calculations. First answer that came to me was what I put down. Hoped I hadn't done that to show off. Probably not— my brain wasn't all together.

The two uniforms herded us into a big locker room. It reminded me of PE. The guy wearing the odd hat said, "Strip down to your underwear and use any locker for your other clothes. When you're done, come through the red doors to the physical testing stations. Be quick about it!"

I sat on a bench in front of a locker, gathering myself. Just had to go through with it. No other way out. On the other side of the red doors, some had shorts and T-shirts, some had just shorts, and then there was me, purposely without either.

I got laughs, and people pointed fingers, but no real nasty remarks. Underwear or not, I was still six feet, four inches and somewhat in shape.

My height didn't deter the uniform wearing the odd hat. "Where's your underwear?"

"I don't wear them, sir. They interfere with circulation around my vital organs."

Laughter broke out again.

I thought I saw the hat jump when he roared, "Silence!" Then, he said through gritted teeth, "Get your pants on."

Again, I got to stick out.

A man in a white coat took me to the first station—a room divided in two by a low wall with a glass partition at chest level. "Sit down and put those earphones on. Each time you hear a beep, press the button in front of you. I'll be in the other half of the room." He shut the door and went around to the other side. I forgot the instructions and put on the headphones, but there was no music, so I made up a beat to go with some lyrics that seemed brilliant at the time:

Ho, Ho, ho Chi Minh

Ho, Ho, hocheeeeeeeee Minh

Ho, hocheee Minh

Pressing the button at every *Minh*.

The operator almost blew my ears out with an angry repetition of the instructions.

I was no dummy, though. I discreetly unplugged the earphones to guard against any future volume shifts and hit the button with every *Minh*.

Next station was for optometry, and I had to wait in a little folding chair next to some farmers. They shoveled some verbal manure my way, and I thought about asking if their mother ironed their underwear—but I was on total discipline. Another man in a white coat asked to see my glasses and said that I'd have to take the tests both with and without them. "Read the smallest line that you can see clearly."

"I'm sorry sir, but I can't make out the words. You must have given me the Hungarian version."

"There is no Hungarian version; this is the English version. Just read the letters one by one."

"Yes sir, but when we're done, will you tell me what the word means?"

"There is no word!"

"But you told me it was in English."

"Just read the letters!"

"T…E…P…O…L…F…D…Z… Are you sure that isn't Hungarian?"

"Just forget languages! Focus on *the letters*!"

"Yes, sir!"

"Now try it without your glasses. Just read the smallest line you can see clearly."

"I think this one's in Italian."

Something snapped. Maybe it was his pencil. It couldn't have been one of his fingers. "Just read the individual letters."

"P…T…E…O."

"You can go now. Please go!"

At the next station, I had to submit to a whole lot of probing and touching by a nurse, while a doctor asked the surfer next to me all sorts of questions. Then he gave me the same ones but also added some. "Are you sexually active?"

"What does active mean?"

"Do you have sexual relations?"

"With whom?"

He raised his voice. "With the opposite sex!"

"Sure."

Another teeth grinder. "Have you ever contracted a venereal disease?"

"Contracted? I don't understand. Sign a contract?"

"No. Have you ever had a venereal disease?"

"I had the clap once. Still don't know who gave it to me. Narrowed it down to three or four." That wasn't really true. I knew who it was.

His lips tightened, and he asked, "Are you on drugs, Mr. Stenrud?"

"No." The psilocybin must have worn off by now.

My next stop was the shrink. I dressed first, taking my time, but had to wait in a corridor. I just shut my eyes and focused on what I thought he would want from me. Some guy in a sport coat with too many patterns opened a door and called me in. I thought maybe I'd be allowed to lie down on a sofa. But no, there was only a metal chair across the desk from him. He had a wooden swivel chair.

"Mr. Stenrud, neither here, nor in my regular practice, have I had a specimen as interesting as you."

That got my attention.

"I can see that a light has gone off in your head," he continued, raising his chin a notch. "Your lack of underwear was not that remarkable, but surely you knew it would garner some curiosity." Stone-faced, he looked straight into my eyes and then opened the test booklet and my answer sheet. "We score these with a template, so your abysmal 32 percent on the verbal might have gone unnoticed, even with your 89 percent on the math. But your attire already made me curious. I examined your verbal answers, and I must say, your approach to the test is completely novel and probably accurate, assuming I interpreted your coding properly."

I started to speak and thought better of it. He waved me off anyway.

"Whether I have your coding right or not is immaterial because it will go nowhere, other than a cocktail party anecdote for me. As goes for your amusing performance with the optometrist." He got out of his chair and leaned into the side of his desk, peering down at me with his bald head, big eyebrows, and smoke-stained teeth.

"The question is simple: are you more trouble to the army than you're worth?" He rubbed his jaw and narrowed his brown eyes at me. "If I could guarantee you'd end up deep in the jungle or in the stockade, I'd be thrilled to recommend 1A." He walked back around the desk and sat down again. He seemed to enjoy taking his time, trying to torture me with his tawdry suspense.

"Unfortunately," he went on, "you're too smart to end up in the stockade and probably too smart to get assigned to combat. You'd just undermine the war effort from some cushy spot." He took his time lighting a thoroughly legal and very smelly cigar before delivering his verdict. "4F! Now get the hell out of my office and go wait in front of room twenty-two for the board's decision."

More of those metal chairs awaited me in front of room twenty-two. I sat on the floor, thinking through anything they might ask.

A civilian barked at me, "Why are you sitting on the floor? Never mind. Come in here." Inside the room, he sat behind a table with four other hairless White men in white shirts and clip-on ties. No, wait. One of them had a bolo tie. That was kind of cool.

I looked around, but there was no chair for me. Thought about sitting on the floor, but being so close to the goal, I knew I'd better not press it. I began to ask for a chair when the guy in the middle started talking. "There is no greater glory than serving in the armed forces of the United States of America. Our country is here because of those men who served before and those serving today. You, Mr. Stenrud, will never have that honor because you are a complete disgrace. You are classified 4F." Unanimous frowns conveyed their total disgust. "Do you have anything to say for yourself?"

"No, sir." I felt like leaping up and running out of there, but I slouched out as they expected.

***

Back at the motel, I showered gloriously, dressed, and felt incredible until I saw the phone book on the desk. Had to get out of the room. I hurried to the airport. Checked in and sat by the gate, remembering Lauren and how I'd changed after those few days with her. I started writing her a letter.

They called my name, and I realized they'd already boarded most of the plane. I almost handed the gate agent the letter I was writing but fumbled and found the ticket. The plane wasn't full; I had a row to myself. After takeoff, a stewardess—brown ponytail held high up the back of her head, wide smiling mouth, and alert, green eyes—asked, "Would you like anything to drink, sir?"

She was worth a conversation, but I just asked for water and spent the flight writing and revising. I finished it before landing in San Francisco and dropped it in a mailbox at the terminal. I felt an incredible release, even more than after the draft physical.

Lauren,

In San Francisco, I took a cab from the airport and had the driver drop me off at the bowling alley on Haight. I wanted to find some of the cats, especially Karl, and tell them my story, but they weren't there. Too drained to look for them anywhere else, I carried my small bag down Stanyan, toward the Panhandle, through the drizzle and cold, wishing I'd brought a different jacket. As I stepped off the pavement at Oak Street, a Chevy stopped in front of me. The driver leaned toward the open passenger window. "Hey Mark. It's Stewie. Got something for you."

Fuck. It's MacFarlane. The cat was a downer even before he was busted. I wanted nothing to do with him. "Stewie, I'm really beat. Need to catch some sleep. Later."

"No, Mark! I got information for you."

I couldn't trust any information from him, but somehow, it hooked me. I sat in the front seat, putting my bag down between us. He drove off, and then I felt it—cold, solid metal pressed into the hair on my neck and a noticeably shaking voice from the backseat, "Don't move around, asshole." As he spoke, I felt little tremors from his gun hand reverberating into the skin of my neck.

My breathing went to a standstill, and numbness spread through my body. Just the right combination. "I won't."

MacFarlane turned right on Shrader, pulled up, and rifled my bag. There was nothing there he wanted. "Where's the fucking stuff, shithead?"

"Just flew back from Phoenix. Those are my clothes from the trip." Damn, I was the calmest one in the car. "I got about eighty bucks."

Gun Man still had the tremors. "Give it to me."

"Okay. I'm going to reach into my pocket. My shirt pocket."

"Stewie, watch him."

I pulled out my cash from my left shirt pocket and held it up.

Gun Man snatched it and counted. "Eighty-six! Where's your wallet?"

"Don't carry one. My license is in the same pocket."

"Search him!" Gun Man ordered.

Stewie frisked me. "Son of a bitch's got nothing more."

Gun Man scratched my neck with the cold metal. "Stewie said you were some big fucking dealer."

"Everybody around here's a dealer."

MacFarlane fixed me in a dumb stare.

"I've given you all I have. Can I go?"

"Open the door slow. If you turn around, I'll shoot your brains out."

I opened the door and kept my right hand on the edge. "I'm looking away. I'll shut the door with my back." I got out with my left hand holding my bag.

They drove off, and I crouched behind a parked car. When they reached the middle of the block, I sprinted away through light traffic on Oak. Stopped in the Panhandle to look back but couldn't tell one set of headlights or taillights from another, so I raced across Fell.

Had my key ready and sat on the inside landing. Stretched out to my full length along the stairs and almost cried. Eighty bucks was nothing, but I'd never had a gun on me before. I went through my bag. The olive shirt Lauren bought me was in there, but one of my desert boots was missing, the other now rendered useless. Zipped the bag and went upstairs.

Marie and Linda were laughing and talking behind Linda's door, but it was best to leave them when their door was shut. Jack sat at the table in the kitchen, wearing a dark blue robe with a little shine to it. He hadn't shaved, but his long black hair was tended.

He smiled. "Hey man. How'd the physical go?"

"4F!"

"Totally far out. I'll open a bottle." Second to banging any willing chick, he had a thing for wine, and he didn't mind if the rest of us took a bottle now and then. But mostly, he liked to show off his collection and drink with you.

He cradled one from the pantry. "This baby is a seven-year-old Bordeaux." He poured us each about a third of a glass and found some leftover sourdough bread and cheese.

This one was smooth, with flavors of red fruit, a very agreeable wine to come down from my first stickup. I didn't want to tell Jack about it. Didn't want to tell anyone but Tony. Had to keep up the aura. I'd just spread the word that MacFarlane was boosting people with a gun-toting junkie.

Jack wouldn't ask me much about the physical. He wasn't that interested in anybody besides himself. I had to start any conversation. At any rate, I wondered what he was doing here chickless. "What are you doing staying home alone?"

"Taking a break, man." He was drinking the wine but just used the bread as a little bulldozer to move pieces of cheese around his plate. "People don't get what a load it is to spend your days doing what I do. Having to talk with so many chicks. Someone said you ought to walk a mile in the other person's boots before you can understand them."

Was he serious or jerking me off? "Maybe you should get an apprentice to give you a break now and then."

"Yeah, maybe he could do my laundry, and I could get him a peephole. Say, I had a chick here the other day, and she remembered this place and you. Said you were a totally far-out fuck."

"She said that after she balled you?"

"Before! You asshole! Anyway, an old girlfriend called me. She's really loaded. I know you think I'm rich, but this chick's family's really rolling in it. She's coming out from New York in a couple of weeks with a friend. They'll be looking for a good time. You'd be great to hang out with them. She'll blow lots of bread on whatever we want."

Seemed like a good idea. "Sure man. Let me know when it's coming up."

I went off to my room, emptied out my bag, held out my solitary desert boot, and looked at my other neatly lined up shoes.

Florida, 1962

On my way to junior high, my sock kept poking out through the hole in my right shoe. I had to keep stopping to adjust the piece of paper bag I'd put there to keep it in. Should have glued it.

Before Florida, I had to pay attention in class. The nuns at my former school, Our Lady of Perpetual Misery, whacked me with finely honed rulers for mistakes, taking religious relish in each swat—and extra relish after Mother divorced. But in Florida, Mother put me in a public school. One-half of the school was Black one-half white, and then there was me, the one Yankee. One-half didn't talk to the other, and, for the most part, neither half talked to me.

The geography monitor in first period had a long stick and walked around the room, pointing to places on his maps. I knew how to say the names of some places in other countries. He didn't at all. Once I corrected him and got a whack from his pointer. Almost every day, he'd give us a quiz. We'd get twenty minutes for a quiz that took even the slowest students fifteen. He'd relax at his desk, looking at the girls he'd placed in the front row.

The bell rang, and I went to civics. Nuns had taught this, too. The monitor was a skinny man with a buzz cut and suspenders. He always read from the textbook, but his voice was soft, and you had to strain to hear him, so I didn't bother.

After homeroom came recess, and with it came another kind of lesson. I hadn't known bullies in Delaware. I didn't have many friends, but nobody bothered me. In stupid Florida, I was the Yankee, and Billy Snomes was my tormentor. There was no hiding from him outside. The library was safe, but they always closed it at recess.

Snomes caught me near a water fountain and backed me against the wall with his beefy arms. Grinning under dim eyes, he slapped me on one side of the face and then the other. He shook himself, but his black hair didn't move. Then came a punch to my chest. "Shitty Yankee!" Another punch.

I was numb. Nothing hurt. The bell rang, and he laughed and kicked my leg.

My English teacher had a beehive hairdo, lots of bracelets, and a bright yellow dress. She didn't understand grammar the way the nuns did.

The bell rang for geometry. I sat in the back. Every day, Mr. Jones called on students for answers, but after the first few days, he didn't call on me anymore. The bell rang for the end of the school day, and I ran to the library, where I found a copy of *McTeague* by Frank Norris.

I walked home, not caring anymore about my protruding sock. Five minutes along, two Black kids stopped in front of me with friendly nods and introduced themselves—Terrell was taller, light brown, and had short hair, while Melvin was darker and just a little shorter.

Terrell asked, "Why're you letting Snomes beat up on you?"

"What?" Why was he asking this?

He said, "We see it every day. He finds you outside and toys with you. You're bigger. Why don't you fight him?"

"Never learned how."

They looked at each other, and Melvin looked back at me and said, "You got to learn to fight. He'll keep beating on you until some other cracker takes over."

What was I supposed to say?

"We're going to show you some things. Come on."

We went into a deserted yard, and they threw crosses, or that was what they called them. Terrell stood at an angle to Melvin and looped his fist at Melvin's outstretched hand. He made it snap as the fist connected. Then it was my turn, and I punched Terrell's hand. They fixed and fixed my punching until I made snaps. Then we worked to protect my face with a high left hand and used it as a jab. I was a good pupil, and we kept at it until Melvin said, "We have to go now. You need to practice. Use a pillow or something."

I was more shocked at them helping me than I was to discover bullying. "Why're you helping me?"

Melvin said, "You're about the only one here that doesn't look at us like they do."

***

I opened the front door to our half of the duplex and put my books on the kitchen table. Mother hadn't left a note. She'd probably be late. Turned on the oven and finished my homework. Ate a TV dinner of Salisbury steak, recognizable corn, and some green stuff. Dinner didn't take long, and I looked for a place that was shoulder height, where I could jam pillows. I couldn't find one in my room or the kitchen. I went into Mother's room with her dripping paintings, jewelry boxes, and large, neatly made bed. Dresses, pants, coats, and blouses in all the colors I knew hung in the closet. Then I saw them: shoe organizers hanging off the inside of the closet doors. I counted twenty-two pairs—different colors, small heels, big heels, some with no heels, shoes, boots, sandals, straps, and no straps. Studied the hole in my right shoe. The left was about to have one too.

Really needed to punch. I stuffed pillows into her closet shelf and went back to it, throwing crosses into the pillows and jabs into the sticky air.

I didn't hear her car or the front door and stood there like a pillar of salt when the bedroom door opened. She came in alone, in her ruffled white blouse, peach skirt, and high heels. "What are you doing in here… What do you have that fist for?"

I unclenched and was temporarily mute.

Her voice rose. "What are you doing in here?"

"I was practicing my right cross and left jab and needed a place to jam the pillows." I pulled them out of her closet.

"I don't want you in here when I'm not home."

I took off my right shoe. "I need new shoes. I showed you these last week."

"You'll have to wait."

"You have twenty-two pairs, and I've got one pair with a big hole."

"You ungrateful brat!" She threw her purse at me. That wasn't all. I'd unleashed it again—the screaming, exaggerating everything she could remember I'd ever done wrong, and imagining things I'd never done. I was the cause of all her hardship. Nothing I'd ever done was forgiven; even the things I hadn't done were never forgiven.

"Get out of here. And you better apologize before breakfast, or I'm leaving, and you can fend for yourself."

I wasn't excited. Couldn't remember the last time I'd gotten upset with her. I just went to bed.

In the morning, I made a glass of Tang and ate dry cereal for breakfast. Left early for school, leaving a note—

Mother,

I give you my completely helpless apology.

Mark

We had a pop quiz in geography. The teacher said it was hard, so we'd have the whole period for it. All we had to do was fill in the capital of each state. I finished and thought about Billy Snomes, especially his face. Yesterday, he had a pimple with a hint of white on his left cheek. I spent civics class thinking about my upcoming meeting with destiny and what all the possible consequences of my crime would be. Then homeroom came, and I forgot all about it while reading *McTeague.*

The bell rang for recess, and I couldn't stop myself from walking faster than normal to the fields and basketball courts. Billy had two friends with him—a high haired, wide bottomed girl and a Brilliantine haired boy.

Billy pushed me against a fence. "We're going to have some real fun today, Yankee." He slapped me twice in the face and shared a laugh with the two dolts. I froze. I couldn't do it. He turned back to me and hit me in the stomach. The boy laughed, and Billy turned his head to him. I wanted to do it. The pimple came into focus—not yet oozing, just white-topped.

Snap!

I'd put more force into it than I'd meant, almost losing my balance, and I wasn't ready with my left. But it didn't matter. Billy dropped to the ground, mouth drooling, eyes fearful. The boy stepped back, dumbstruck, and the girl shrieked. Other students hurried over. I wasn't interested at all in beating people up or bragging about it, so I left, but I knew now about my strong right hand.

Teacher came over. Kids said the Yankee did it, but he told them they'd need a better story than that.

Lagunitas

I found Linda and Renee standing on the front steps of our building: Linda sporting a red beret above her blue-green, wool poncho and Renee closed tight in an embroidered sheepskin coat, protecting her against the April wind and cold. She gave me a kiss and asked, "Did you know Tony's dropping tonight?" The kiss was not as warm as I'd expected, and I hoped I'd still be able to use the four Moby Grape tickets in my pocket.

"Tried to talk him out of it."

We'd all dropped for concerts before. One time had been great for me, and another way too freaky. So much could happen in the ballroom with so many people dancing and stomping and with lights flashing. I tried to talk him out of it, but he, so cool and careful all the time, just wanted to let loose tonight. He'd be fine with me watching, but that would sure limit my possibilities.

He delicately opened his flat's front door with his shoulders stooped, mouth agape, and head of bushy black hair rocking slowly side to side. "Wow. Air."

Renee nudged his shoulder. "Cut it out. You only just dropped." She was pissed, and so was I really. Finally, a night with Renee—and now this. Tony straightened, and we all laughed, but it wouldn't be long now. I'd just have to stay close and keep him away from trouble.

Linda asked, "Where's the car?"

"Around the block." I'd assumed we'd all walk to it, but with the girls upset, I tried the Cary Grant route. "I'll get it."

I brought Jack's car around. Made sure no one was behind me and stopped in front of our building with the turn signals on. The girls watched Tony get in front and slid into the back seat. I saw them talking softly in the rearview mirror. Maybe they were plotting a new adventure, given they couldn't count on me and Tony anymore.

I wondered whether I should take the back streets with all the stop signs or get on the one-ways with the traffic. Toss up as to which would be easier on Tony. Took the one-ways.

Traffic light half a block ahead of us switched to red, and a wall of cars sent brake lights flashing across all three lanes. Tony sank back into his seat and then edged forward, index finger outstretched and arcing across the windshield. "Red! Red lights! Red lights, man."

After that, I tried to stay back from clumps of traffic to avoid another brake light show. I miscalculated, and a stoplight sent brake lights into vibrant red across three lanes. Tony swept his arm vigorously and told us in that deep, low voice, "Same thing, man! All that red. Stopping red!"

At least the girls tried to control their laughter. He pivoted his head toward the backseat, his index finger having found a new attraction—Linda's beret. "Red."

Linda corrected him. "No, it's burgundy, Tony."

I wondered why she needed to say that, but it didn't bother him.

Near the Carousel Ballroom, I looked for parking. Didn't see any and asked the girls, "Do you want me to drop you off and find you later?"

They used some silent female signaling, and Renee said, "We'll stay with you for now."

I turned into an area filled with warehouses and small factories and found a spot in front of a series of one-story, glass-walled buildings.

I hustled around to the passenger side. Tony had gotten out by himself but was immobilized, totally transfixed by what was behind the glass. The lights were on inside, and you could see lots of equipment—pipes, big vessels, valves, levers, and gauges extended from one building to the next. Signs stood at the roofline of each building. Directly in front of us—Plastics Factory #5. Next was #4, and I thought I could make out #3.

I followed Tony as he broke off down the street. He made it to the last of the series of buildings—Plastics Factory #1. Then eased back toward me, waiting in front of #3.

He spoke as if underwater, eyes totally agog. "The numbers were going the wrong way."

"But you fixed it, man." I put an arm around his shoulder. "Let's walk up to #5, and you can fix it some more. Renee and Linda are up there."

He looked up the street and walked; his eyes surveyed the numbers. He got to the girls by Factory #5, and he said, with his voice still underwater, "We fixed it."

The girls stood next to each other: Renee's head rolling and Linda's hand in front of her mouth.

Tony strode up to the factory. He peered in, turned around, and said, "PLASTICS!"

Now the chicks couldn't control their laughter, and it was hard to blame them.

I put my arm around him again and said, "Tony, we're going to the concert. Can we see this later?" I tried pulling on his jacket to get him away from the glass.

I got him away for a moment, but he said, "No man. *Plastics.*" He turned right back, scanning all around the factory.

The girls sidled over to me, and Renee said, "Sorry, Mark. This isn't working."

"I know." I gave them their tickets.

"Maybe we'll see you inside," she said.

"Maybe."

They walked off, but before they'd gone far, I remembered what I was holding and called them back. "I have to be safe if I'm alone with him." I handed Renee the joints.

"You're right." She wore the warmest smile I'd ever seen on her. "Sorry Mark. I want to be with you, but I want the music too…"

I looked back at Tony, who was peaceful by the glass wall, and then back to Renee. "It's okay." Two other cats would be happy tonight. I'd chosen my partner and knew it was the right choice.

Went back to Tony, who pointed at the equipment beyond the glass walls. "Pipes, man."

"Yeah, pipes. Pipes, you and me, man."

***

Tony and I had to stop borrowing cars, so we bought one. I had wanted an old Jaguar, and Tony an Italian job, but foreign was too flashy, so we got a four-year-old white Oldsmobile Starfire with bucket seats, subdued fins, and a little less than open-ocean steering. I guess it had a little flash but only the normal American amount.

One cold spring day, we drove downtown to pick up my new glasses—a gold-rimmed regular pair and tortoise shell shades. We were done well before noon and had no pressing needs, so we tooled along in the Starfire, taking in the sights on the way back to the Haight.

Tony stopped for a light in a dicey area outside of downtown. Up ahead, two skinny blonds in short skirts leaned against a wall. One had a bikini top, and the other had a rolled-up blouse. Lucky for them, the sun was out on their side of the street. They reminded me of a debt I owed from my first day in San Francisco. "Tony, let's park. I want to talk with those chicks."

"What are you going to talk to them about? Politics?"

"It's important to me."

"Hell, they'll charge you to talk."

"We've got nothing going on today."

He relented. "All right, but I'll just watch."

"We aren't holding?" I asked.

"Nothing but the two joints you've got."

We parked on the next block and walked back. "Good morning, ladies." One had a marginal smile, and the other had a small bruise on her right cheek. "I'm Mark, and this is Tony."

The barely smiling one said, "We don't need to know your names." She gave a price for a full and a half but mumbled it, so we didn't get the numbers.

Put my shades in a jacket pocket, so they could see my eyes. "You could take a ride with us, and we could work it all out."

"We got to work it out *first*."

"We're sort of into a lot of foreplay. How's that work with a full and a half?" They hadn't done a lot of negotiating and didn't know what to say, so I kept going. "Didn't I see you girls at the bus station yesterday?"

"We came in last week."

"Tony and I could show you the hip places, the ones with lots of cool people. Bet that's what you came out here to see."

They were interested but hesitant. "Maybe later. We have to work."

A guy named Freddy showed up, decked out in a purple coat that might've been a cape. "You fucking ass hippy motherfuckers. You're scaring away the customers."

I gave him my earnest smile. "We are customers."

"You sure got one dumb smile."

I had on a red plaid western shirt with pearl-colored snap buttons on the flaps over the chest pockets. I unsnapped one, took out an evenly rolled joint, and offered it to him in my cupped hand. "We're all about peace and love, man."

He squeezed the joint between his thumb and forefinger and drew it across his nose. His shoulders relaxed, and he put the joint in a coat pocket. "What are you doing here with my girls when you got all that free love up there in that Haight-Ashbury?"

I handed him the other joint for good measure and looked back at the girls, who were getting cold with the fog now rolling in overhead. "Lust man. Lust at first sight!"

His forehead scrunched. "Wendy, ain't you told him the price?"

I helped her out. "She did, but we want a different price."

"What the fuck you mean?"

"What's the all-night price?"

"All night? It ain't yet lunch time." He spat on the sidewalk but not near Tony or me.

"Call it the all-day and all-night price." I couldn't see his eyes behind the sunglasses, but his head pivoted toward me, and I put my shades back on. "We're not your straight johns. We want to do some righteous balling with Wendy and— What's her friend's name?"

"Dawn."

"They'll come back to you purring like kittens."

"You ain't got enough dick to make my ladies purr!"

I unzipped and pulled it out.

"Put that back, you crazy-ass motherfucker! You want the heat over here?"

Readjusting my corduroys, I said, "Big enough?"

Freddie mulled a response. The girls' faces had gone blank. Tony shuffled between Dawn and me, and I knew I'd have to get this over with before he busted clean through laugh control.

"So, how much for all night?" I asked.

"Five hundred a piece."

"A thousand! Fuck man. That's half a new VW. No way. Two bills total."

"You sure talk a lot, and you got no green. You trying to con me?"

Time to show a little ego. "That's really uncool, man. You think I'm so stupid, so fucking stupid that I'd try and con a pimp, a San Francisco pimp. That's really insulting."

"You got some thin skin, thin white skin. Fucking crazy-ass hippy." He looked at Tony, Dawn, Wendy, and finally at me. "Four bills."

We settled on two fifty, and I slipped Freddy the bread. He left after a couple of long looks at the girls.

Tony asked them, "You girls have any more clothes? We'll be gone all night."

Wendy said, "In our room at the hotel around the corner."

It wasn't really a hotel, just a four-story brick building with dirty shades flapping in the open windows. The few people nodding off in the lobby were easy with sad smells and broken furniture. The girls didn't even try the elevator. After heading up two flights, Dawn put a finger to her lips and opened a door. Four mattresses on the floor, one occupied by a blanket-clutching shape with tangled hair.

As the girls went in, Tony pulled me from the door and whispered, "Okay, what are we going to do with them?"

"Don't know, but we should get them out of the city."

"How about Carlos and Annie's?" Tony offered.

"Great idea!"

"All right, but let's get going. I'll bring the car around."

Wendy and Dawn came out with a duffel bag. Wendy asked, "Where's your friend?"

"He's getting the car. Let me carry that." That got a nice rise out of them, and they let me. Tony pulled up as we came out of the building. I sat in the back with Wendy, and Dawn went up front.

We drove up Haight and toward Stanyan, so they could check out the scene and awe at what the fashionable chicks wore—bell-bottoms, leathers, shawls, granny dresses, peasant blouses, leather jackets, headbands, and knee-length boots. They spared longer looks for the new arrivals sitting on the pavement. Freddy had saved them from that.

A shriek from Dawn jerked me out of my thoughts. "Wendy, there's a bowling alley!"

"We got to stop! Please. Please! We'll do anything for you."

They begged, offering us anything and everything and forgetting that technically we were already entitled to everything.

Tony parked, and they hurried off to Park Bowl. Didn't take long for them to stroll back, talking to each other and cooking up some plot.

Wendy said, "It's not fair! We haven't been bowling in weeks, and it's closed. Dawn and I were champions back home." She looked at Dawn for encouragement and went on. "But we saw some dress shops, and we need a few things."

"Need a few things?" Tony asked.

"A few things!" Dawn insisted.

Tony put an arm around her, leaned her back with one hand on her bottom, and kissed her righteously. Wendy had her own little ways and sidled up to my right side, chin down, and eyes up, rubbing a breast on my upper arm.

Damn. We were an easy touch. We walked to the nearest shop and gave them sixty dollars. They came out with a granny dress for Dawn and bell-bottoms and a flowery blouse for Wendy. "How do we look?" They did a few turns. "We've got sweaters in the bag and some change."

Wasn't much change, but they'd fit in a lot better now. We stopped near our building on Fell, and Tony ran in for supplies. Memories of the backseat with Lauren got in the way, so I took the driver's seat. Wendy and Dawn looked confused but stayed put. When Tony came down, he didn't hesitate, just hopped in back and engaged with Wendy.

Going over the Golden Gate Bridge, Dawn was excited as a cheerleader at homecoming—wide eyed and taking in the bay, the bridge, and Alcatraz.

When we entered the Waldo Tunnel, she asked, "What's your sign?"

"Positive." That didn't click with her. I had better play the game. "Sagittarius."

"I knew it. I totally knew it. You're so out front. So *there*. Really, completely there."

"How about you?"

"Guess."

"Give me a clue."

"I'm a water sign."

"Aquarius."

"That's an air sign."

Damn. I thought Aquarius was like an aquarium. "Pisces." That sounded fishy.

"How'd you guess?"

"Just lucky."

"I'm going to get my stars done."

I didn't know anything about that and asked, "So, where are you from?"

"Minnesota."

"Wendy, too?"

"Yeah."

"Minneapolis?"

"No, I grew up on a farm outside Rochester. Wendy and I went to school together."

I started to ask why they left but caught myself. Some of those stories were too painful. And anyway, she was daydreaming. In about two hours, we turned down the road to the place with a trunk full of the groceries we'd picked up. Trees spread all over—mostly apple—and two houses, one with two stories, a big porch, a barn, and some sheds. A peace flag and a United Nations flag reigned over an unruly vegetable garden. We carried the food into the main house, but nobody was there.

Music floated up from the river, and we started toward the sounds. Soon, we saw Carlos with his easy walk and fat mustache. Tony gave the chicks two joints and said, "You can make friends with these. We'll catch up with you."

They hesitated, but the music drew them away.

Carlos smiled at them as they went by. "Long time since I've seen you two cats."

"We brought groceries and this." Tony handed him a baggy with about twenty-five tabs of acid.

"And two chicks," I said. "Rescued from the streets of San Francisco."

"Rescued? What do you mean?" I could see it dawning on him. He broke up laughing. "You mean they're hookers?" He sat at a picnic table near the back door and picked an apple from a bowl on the table.

I sat across from him. "Don't think they were on the street long. They couldn't say their price aloud. They mumbled it. Said they came in by bus last week."

Carlos stopped laughing and asked, "Are you still building up your good karma, Mark?"

Tony said, "He's moved on to being a fucking social worker." He started toward the river. "I'm going to see how they're doing down there."

"Would you like two volunteers?" I asked. "They're farm girls. Probably know more about gardening than anybody here."

Carlos was either thinking it over or waiting for me to sweeten the pot. No, he was a decent cat. He was just thinking.

"What's wrong with two good-looking farm girls who were on the street for a little?" I asked.

"The clap for one thing."

"You can get the clap from anyone that shows up here." Laughter drifted up from the river. "You still have that doctor here?"

"You need him?"

"No, we're fine, but he can check them."

"Yeah, he'll give them a complete physical." He laughed again.

"So, we're okay."

"Sure, Mark. We're okay. You guys are two cool cats."

Tony came back. "They're skinny dipping."

When I stood up to go, Carlos asked, "You going to say goodbye to them?"

"Should we?"

"I can tell them you had to bail somebody out." He held up the baggy of tablets. "We'll drop tonight, and they'll forget all about you."

As the three of us walked out to the Olds, Carlos said, "Say, if you're looking to get out of the city, there's a place in Lagunitas that needs some major rent help. It's an old summer lodge at the end of a road—big deck, trees all around, and no neighbors nearby. They say it was Teddy Roosevelt's, but they say that about every big house at the end of a road over there."

Major rent help meant anybody with any money had moved out, the rent was due, and the remaining people felt they had some rights due to long-term occupancy. But after Stewie MacFarlane and his junkie friend, I could consider suburban living. "What do you think, Tony?"

"Maybe. Who's there now, Carlos?"

"Two or three. Good people. Danny's the one I know. There's a general store on Sir Francis Drake and a restaurant on the other side of the road. Scandinavian, I think. Just right for Mark. Take the road by the restaurant to the end. The rent is maybe three hundred."

We said our goodbyes and decided to give Lagunitas a look. Tony knew a place for sandwiches in Petaluma, but he wanted to avoid his family or anyone else he knew. So, I got them, and we ate, driving hilly, almost empty back roads.

After Tony finished, he said, "Those chicks were partying so much in the river. I almost jumped in."

"Cool, cautious Tony jumping in naked! Holy cow, man. You might become a hippy soon."

"Fuck you!"

"At least they can leave there whenever they want and fuck whoever they want."

"What gave you the idea?"

"When I saw them on the street, I remembered coming into San Francisco and sitting at the bus station for a long time, studying a map and collecting my thoughts. Saw some chicks come in, two together and two by themselves. Something like that. Each time, there were men on them like hawks. I was so new; I didn't figure out what was going on until later. Then I felt like a total ass for not doing anything."

"What the hell could you do?"

"I don't know about then, but we did it now!"

"And I owe you half the pimp money. But say, pulling it out on the street wasn't the wisest."

"I know, but he was the only one holding. I'd already given him the joints. Fucking pimp!"

We laughed so hard that we almost had to pull over.

I handed Tony half of the brownie from the store and asked, "You know Lagunitas?"

"No. Only driven through. It's not really a town, just a bunch of houses spread up in the hills. Most of them are deep in the forest."

We took a right at Sir Francis Drake and drove past a bar and a post office before we saw the general store and restaurant. From there, the road wound up through the forest with houses set back off the road. A few dogs ran and barked at us but lost interest, leaving us with the sounds of birds and the wind moving through high branches. The road narrowed, coming to a dead end with a big wooden lodge of at least two stories on the left. There was a large open garage with a pickup and a partially disassembled sports car, a huge Argentinian propane tank, and a deck half the size of a basketball court sat on top of the garage. Up the stairs and left of the garage, a large open doorway beckoned.

Before we could knock, a cat came out. Barefoot, jeans, embroidered vest, and no shirt. Long blond hair, flat around his face. Didn't look like he'd ever needed to shave.

"I'm Mark, and this is Tony. Carlos in Guerneville sent us. Said to ask for Danny."

"That's me."

Tony said, "Maybe we can help with the rent."

Danny gestured to the big deck. Bench seating extended around three sides. Backboards gave you something to lean against, and a narrow top board acted as a place to rest things on or sit on if you didn't have too large of a butt.

"We need more than help. What you cats do? Musicians? Dealers?"

Tony adjusted his sunglasses. "Acid. But in the city, not here."

I added, "We'd be commuters. Go to the city for business, have a martini, and come home."

Danny wasn't yet interested in humor. "You'd be holding here?"

Tony said, "Now and then, but we move it on. And we deliver. Nobody comes to us."

Danny lit a joint and passed it on. "You can take care of the rent and help with the food?"

I nodded and asked, "Who's here beside you?"

"A guy named Bill and my sort of old lady, Rachel. We're into macrobiotics, but we'll cook most anything."

We did a tour. You could fit eight Oldsmobiles in the living room and a VW bug in the stone fireplace. There were a couple of big couches, along with lots of pillows on the floor. Not much decoration, just a stuffed moose head on the wall. Kitchen and bathroom downstairs. Shower didn't look that great. And of all things, a walk-in safe. Nobody knew the combination, but Bill crashed in it when he was here, which apparently wasn't all that often. The bedrooms were on the second floor. Tony took the one on the other side from the deck. I chose the cabin in the back. It was small, but I liked that. I could imagine being a monk with few possessions—just my clothes, books, and a writing desk.

***

When I made it to the kitchen in the morning, Tony sat at the table with Rachel, who asked, "Pancakes?"

"Sure." I followed her to the stove and warmed my hands on a steaming cup of tea.

She was barefoot with a frayed, pink Oxford shirt over billowing striped pajama bottoms. An embroidered headband held her long, red hair that flowed around her freckles and full face. She had some kind of project arranged around the stove.

"What's all that for?" I asked.

"Candles. We use them and sell some. I'll put a couple in the cabin." She handed me a plate of pancakes and pointed to some nut butter on the table. "It's so cool that you and Tony are moving in."

"I like it already. Tony though, I don't know. He's really particular."

"No way. Tony's the easygoing one. You're the intense one."

"Why's everybody always calling me intense?"

"Smile more, and maybe they won't."

I didn't have anything to say to that. Besides, I'd mastered everything about being cool, except for the part about being relaxed. That would take more work than I was putting in.

"Tony said you're going into the city today. Could you bring us some acid? There's a guy across Sir Francis Drake, but he wants five bucks a tab."

"Sure."

She pulled out some crumpled dollar bills. She already knew what we did. She was just being cool.

"Keep the money," I said. "We'll bring you some. What's this guy's name?"

"Bobby. We went to a party at his place once. He's a little creepy, but he's the dealer up here."

"We'll bring acid for the house." She was a real earth mother, and we'd have to keep her happy.

On the way into the city, Tony and I detoured around, checking out our new neighborhood and learning the roads and turnoffs.

"There's a golf course," I said.

"You know how to play?"

"No, but it has to be more interesting than bowling."

"You'd look great in green plaid pants."

"Fuck you." Dressing any way that wasn't low-key had to be reserved for chicks.

We settled back into observing our new environs until I asked, "How we going to do this? I mean, are you going to give up your room on Fell? I think I want to keep mine."

Tony said, "We need a place in the city, so we can break the batch into lots when you come over from Berkeley. You don't want to drive all the way back to Lagunitas, break it up, and drive into the city. And we'll need a place to hang out in the city, so we can keep our eyes and ears open."

"Maybe we can share one."

"Let's think about that. Say, I saw that prick Dave. He tried to slink away and gave me some story. We shouldn't have fronted him anything. I know you think he's a friend, but that's done. He's bad news."

When I first came to the city, I tried selling newspapers. The first time I'd gotten copies of *the Oracle* and *the Barb* at the Print Mint to sell, they sent me out with Dave. I was useless at selling them. Maybe I looked too hungry and scary those first weeks. But he'd sell his and mine too, picking up chicks along the way. He specialized in downtown secretaries—plump ones, sad ones. I'd felt some loyalty to him because of the tiny cut he'd given me for selling my papers. "You're right. That was a mistake, but let's try once more. It is five hundred dollars. Is he still on Lyon?"

"Think so, but he could move anytime."

About eleven, we made it to his place—a run-down Queen Anne. Someone Tony vaguely knew answered the door and let us in. He said Dave was in his room but probably asleep. We got to his door and slipped in with only a slight creak from the unoiled door hinge.

There was little in the room to keep Dave company. A chair. Clothes stacked in a corner. Posters randomly on the walls, and a window with a view of another building only a few feet away. Boots and yesterday's jeans on the floor next to a mattress with a still-sleeping Dave.

I pulled the wallet from his pants, and we peered inside. Three hundred and thirty-four dollars! I took three hundred, put the wallet back, and shook his shoulder until he stirred.

"Fuck. It's early, man." Dave usually spent an hour or more washing his curly, long black hair as if he were always preparing for a Breck commercial. But now, it was greasy.

Tony had never liked him. "Beauty sleep won't help you."

"Fuck you!" Dave sat up, blinking, shrugging, and trying to arrange his hair.

Tony looked down at him while I crouched in front, eye to eye. "Dave, we haven't heard from you. We fronted you those tabs more than a week ago. You owe us five hundred dollars."

"I don't have anything but a few bucks. You know I'm good for it." He pulled his jeans on without checking for his wallet.

Tony said, "We'll take the tabs then."

"I ain't got them, man."

I reached out and put a hand on his knee. "This is pretty heavy. You don't have our money, and you don't have our tabs."

He buried his head in his hands. "I blew it, man. I just fucked up."

Tony said, "Fucked up? Hell, I hear chicks leave your bed in the middle of it." Dave started to say something, but Tony talked over him. "We'll be back in two days, and you better have the cash."

Outside, the fog had temporarily receded, and I put on my shades. Personally, I preferred the fog and the clouds. They nurtured our little psychedelic haven. Going about stoned or coming down was a lot easier when you were out of the bright sunshine.

"What was that about chicks leaving his bed?" I asked.

"I had an uncle, a *ladies' man* they called him. He said the two worst ways to hurt a man were to criticize his screwing or his driving, and Dave doesn't have a car."

Finding the money in his wallet had erased all my sympathy for the prick. "When do you think he'll discover his bread is gone?"

"Total mystery. And when he misses it, he'll have to figure out who took it. Us? His roommates? Or maybe he actually had a chick last night." We headed toward Haight Street. "We covered our costs. Let's forget him."

I agreed. "He's forgotten."

We debated hanging out with some of the cats but instead decided on shopping for our new digs. We bought posters at the Print Mint, gathered our remaining stash and some clothes from Fell Street, and drove to Cost Plus on the wharf for some rugs and blankets. For me, serendipity struck. There was a big display of the same hard candy Julian had given me. Imported from France in all sorts of flavors— cherry, lemon, orange, strawberry, and, most importantly, raspberry. Pastilles, they called them. I bought a carton of the little tins.

We headed back over the Golden Gate and stopped at the Lagunitas general store for groceries. Maple syrup had become critical. Rachel's pancakes were tasty, but with nut butter, it was like eating warm, recently mixed concrete.

A cat was waiting for us outside the store. "You the two who moved into Big Brother's place?" The guy was tanned and muscular with a smile that was not entirely friendly. He had blond, curly hair well over his ears.

Tony said, "Big Brother's been gone a while. Danny's running the place."

He offered us his hand. "I'm Bobby. Why don't you follow me to my place? Got some things to show you."

We figured we may as well get it over with and followed his Mustang convertible east toward Forest Knolls and left up into the bare hills, north of Sir Francis Drake. He had a modern pad with lots of windows and a garage underneath. Up on his wraparound deck, two topless chicks sunbathed face down.

One turned toward us, squinting into the sun. "Bobby, you staying with us now?"

"Sure, babe. Soon as I take care of a little business."

He pulled back a sliding glass door, and we went into a room with a bar, wooden stools, and lots of brightly colored pillows on a carpeted floor. "You cats want a drink or something?"

Tony said, "Thanks man, but we need to go soon. Don't want the groceries to get hot."

Tony and I'd talked about buying some acid, letting him think we weren't in the business. Although, he'd probably find out at some point and get pissed, thinking we'd made a fool of him.

"I can tell you guys are cool, so if you need anything, just let me know. I've got great acid right now for four dollars and fifty cents."

I tried on a mellow smile. "Bobby, we're into the same things, but we're not here to get in your way. We're not doing anything in Marin but relaxing. We're low profile, and we just want to get away from the craziness."

His face twitched as he grasped the situation.

Best to keep talking while he was surprised, so I said, "We're not going to tell anybody about you, and we don't want you talking about us. Low-key and friends. You cool with that?"

Twitching stopped. His calculating brain turned to greed. "If you got a good price for something, I could work with you."

"Sorry. We can't do that. Whole lot of reasons. Just can't do anything in Marin."

Tony threw him a bone. "But if you get some hash or psilocybin…"

"Sure. I get that sometimes." He nodded, seeming like he felt important again. "You want coke or smack?"

I thought Tony was going to read it to him, but he just said, "That shit's over the line, man."

Bobby fidgeted and said, "I know. I know, man, but some people want it."

We started to go, but he had something else for us. "The sheriff is the main heat up here. We used to have this guy who was really hard, but they suspended him because they found naked pictures of him in some magazine."

So what? "They still patrol up here, right?"

"Yeah. I just thought you'd want to know."

Tony said, "Straight people are weird, man." We shook his hand and left him with his dumb look and the sunbaked chicks.

Miranda

It was June, dark and cold as Tony and I drove up to the lodge. Not much of a fire inside. We'd have to buy more wood. Radio was on, and Danny, Rachel, and some other cat I didn't know were listening. All of them somber, dead somber.

"They shot Bobby," cried Rachel.

"Bobby who?" asked Tony.

"Kennedy. They killed him. In LA."

My God, they shot Martin Luther King last month, or maybe it was the month before. No one was smoking, too depressing for that. I went into the kitchen for some wine but couldn't find any. Danny came in, and I asked, "Do we have any wine?"

"No, but I'll get some."

Gave him some cash.

"The guy out there is Ron. Old friend. Musician. Split up from his band. Needs a place to get his act together. There's a room upstairs he can have, the one with windows over the deck."

Tony and I paid the rent, but we really didn't get all that much say. So, I didn't think Danny was really asking me, but I couldn't think about it anyway, said, "okay," and went back in the big room to say hello to Ron. He looked like a decent but sad cat. Maybe that was just for today. Assassinations could do that to you, but we'd probably all forget about it by tomorrow. We'd dropped out after all. I said good night and retreated to my cabin. We had business tomorrow.

***

We left late in the morning, and I dropped Tony in San Rafael for the bus into the city. Drove over the bridge, through treeless stretches of Richmond, and up into Berkeley. I ordered a tea at the coffee house on Euclid, sat by the window, and opened my copy of *Siddhartha*.

Julian walked in and ignored me. I finished my tea and went up to his place. His partner, Francis, let me in, and we went straight to business—cash for him and fifteen hundred tabs for me.

Francis had short black hair, a long nose, and dark, cool eyes. I'd only ever seen him in corduroy pants or khakis, tattersall button-downs, and penny loafers. I wondered what he dressed like when he wasn't trying to look straight.

"Mark, we have to talk about something."

"Okay."

"We need to cut the number of people we deal with. We like you, so you're in, but you're going to have to commit to at least twenty-five hundred from every batch."

I was already losing Jerry and Connie, and we hadn't found any new reliable people. "I'm not sure I can, Francis. I'll have to think about it."

"Don't worry. We know you're friends with Eric in the city. If you can't commit, he'll work with you at a good rate." He stood up and put an arm on my shoulder. "Nothing personal. Just need to make it safer for all of us."

It wasn't personal, just business. I knew he liked *Stranger in a Strange Land,* so I said, "I grok, man."

He laughed. "We'll make it work, Mark."

I left Berkeley with the load and headed to the Bay Bridge, past the mud flats, driftwood sculptures, and anti-war signs. Traffic was light, and the fog was clearing. I liked to pick a car near the toll plaza, get in front of it, and pay for them. It was only an extra fifty cents. I'd pick uptight people, good-looking chicks, and Blacks with hair. It was always good for a laugh, a wave, an evil look, and once a chick named Mona. Not today. I was on total discipline.

Tony was waiting in my flat. I told him about our chemists' plans while we divided the load into four packages—two three-fifties, a five hundred, and a three hundred.

"That's fucking heavy man, and we still haven't gotten anybody to replace Connie and Jerry."

"I know, and we don't need more money or risk, but let's get through today, and we'll figure it out." Had to change the mood and pulled a tin of pastilles from my jacket, holding it out for Tony.

He reached but pulled back when he saw the contents. "Are those acid?"

I laughed. "Blanks. They had a problem with the tablet machine, so they did a test run with just colored binder."

"That is some weird shade of yellow. Color for a bad trip." He stood up from the table. "You keeping them?"

"Souvenir!"

"Stupid souvenir. They could have residue. Besides, even the dumbest cop won't think they're hard candy. He'll think they're acid."

"Maybe." I found my pastille tins in the closet and exchanged the tin of yellow blanks for an unopened, raspberry flavored one.

Jack stopped me on the way out. "Remember the two chicks I know from back East? The ones I said would be great to party with?"

I didn't remember.

"We talked about it after your draft physical. One of the girls is really loaded."

"Oh, yeah!"

Jack rarely looked intense. "We're all meeting up tonight. You still in?"

"Totally, man."

"We'll stay with them, so grab clothes for a few days. We'll leave around six."

When I caught up with Tony on the sidewalk, he asked, "What's up with Jack?"

"Invited me to a party."

Tony looked half offended. "And not me?"

"Only two chicks."

He laughed and rolled his eyes. "Glad I'm not going. That's not even enough for him."

We changed the route for the day, planning to go together to each stop with each of us holding two lots. It would take longer, but we had to vary the routine. The Panhandle was alive with people walking, sitting in circles, juggling, and dancing. Incense all around but the strongest smell was weed. Friends called to us as we walked along, and we'd wave or stop and talk. Tried to stay away from people smoking. We didn't want the smell on us during our runs.

First delivery was quick and easy. Nate and Elin's place was second. They had the ground floor of a three-level Italianate. She opened the door wearing a bright blue T-shirt that reached the top of her hips. She didn't care one way or another about being provocative; she just liked Nate and didn't like clothes. God, she was gorgeous. A Viking princess reborn as a clothes-adverse freak. She and Nate weren't just shacked up; they were locked together, absolutely hung up on each other. You never just heard about Nate or Elin. It was always Elin *and* Nate or Nate *and* Elin. She left us in the living room, her tight cheeks receding from our eager sight.

Most of the house was done up with concert prints and Cost Plus fabrics, but they'd left the living room as it had been with the Russian widow who'd had the place before them. Sturdy lacquered furniture, shawls on coat racks, dusty tea sets, and icons everywhere. The sofa was a roomy worn purple. A big chair had been reupholstered long ago in a pattern that was already out-of-date. The biggest icon in the room caught my eye—a gold painted frame enclosing a Russian-looking Jesus, who was not at all like your typical Italian Jesus. I wondered if I went to Lapland, would Jesus look like a Lapp in a wool cap with earflaps?

Nate eased in—barefoot, jeans, and an untucked lumberjack shirt. He wanted to talk after the business was over. "There's a guy going around trying to buy five thousand tabs. Both people I'd heard it from said he's short and stocky with dark hair just over his ears—and he's got a mustache.

One of my people, Hank, wanted to sell to him, but it felt too weird, and I don't want anything to do with it. I just told him to drop it."

Tony asked, "Did you see this guy?"

"No."

Tony said, "Talking big on the street. Must be a dimwit or a narc looking for greedy people."

Nate agreed. "What can we do? But be careful and tell people to stay away from him."

"You can keep Hank under control?"

He nodded.

Outside, Tony said, "Someday, I'll figure out why she even wears the shirt."

I stopped in my tracks and asked, "What's more important: figuring that out or finally seeing her breasts?"

We laughed, collected ourselves, and headed for Blake's.

We turned onto Frederick Street and spotted trouble right away—a police cruiser and two unmarked cars—double-parked in front of Blake's. Fifteen or so people stood together on the opposite sidewalk. Our bodies wanted to turn and go, but we had to walk up as if the commotion didn't bother us.

We stopped near the crowd, listened, and watched but already knew what was happening.

I asked the nearest cat, "How long has this been going on?"

"Thirty minutes, maybe."

Tony's hands were jammed in his pockets. Sweat formed on his forehead. I didn't want to do anything out of the ordinary and couldn't whisper to him, so I just stood close, breathing slowly. He had to maintain his cool.

The big event for the crowd started. Cops trotted out of the building and down the stairs with two handcuffed freaks—Blake and another cat. They had their heads down and looked only at the sidewalk. Lord, I wished they'd bristle, like wild horses with unwanted ropes on their necks. But no, they were more like sheep as the heat hustled them into the cars and took off.

We walked away.

Tony's voice was low but rapid and edgy. "I can't do this anymore. It's too fucking heavy."

"Hey man, I'm the one still holding. Please keep it together."

We walked in silence for a few blocks.

When he spoke, his voice had slowed. "Meet you back on Fell."

This was awkward as all hell. "Okay."

He walked off easily, and I was fucking alone again. It seemed like right whenever I'd get close to someone, they'd always leave. I started toward Jerry's with eight hundred tabs—his five hundred and Blake's three hundred. Had to check my pace too often. I could deal with holding and with the bust, but Tony was too much. I tried to calm down by naming parked cars—make, model, and year. Didn't get them all right, but it didn't matter. After a few blocks, I could walk, just registering what was around me: cars, trees, types of houses, and people.

Connie let me in and led me down to the workroom. They were already preparing packages—Jerry on a stool, gloves on and writing labels. I told them about Blake, but they didn't know him. I didn't mention the guy wanting five thousand tabs; they wouldn't even sniff at such a thing.

I sat on a stool across from Jerry. "This could be my last load."

He pushed his stool back. "What! Man, we have orders!"

"I've got an extra three hundred now."

"We'll take that, but what the fuck, man!"

Connie moved next to him and put a hand on his shoulder. "Easy, Jerry. We're stopping too. Let's figure this out."

"Sorry, Mark. I'm never calm when I'm down here packaging."

Connie took over. "What's going on, Mark?"

"I can't do this forever. Maybe it's time for me to go to college." Feeling thirsty, I looked around for something to drink.

Connie said, "We know it's getting harder, but we have our budget for law school. We need two more months of this. Is there someone else?"

Jerry said, "Shit, Connie. We're almost done. It's a hell of a time to link up with another supplier."

Now, it was just a problem to solve, and my mind could focus on it. "Hold on," I said. "I have a friend that gets it from the same chemist. We've done each other favors. He moves twice what I do and would probably be happy to have you. If you want, I'll ask him."

Connie asked, "But you aren't sure you're quitting?"

"No, not yet." I thought about asking for water, but I just wanted to leave. "I'll decide in a few days, and if you want, I'll talk to my friend here in the city. Give you enough time to work it out with him."

They looked at each other, and Jerry said, "I guess that's the best we can do."

Connie gave me a surprisingly good kiss, and that was that.

I wanted to amble through Buena Vista Park and collect my thoughts on the way back, but I was holding a lot of bread and stuck to the sidewalks. I'd have to get money to Blake, to help, and to remind him about outlaw loyalty.

I rang Tony's bell, and Renee let me in. Her eyes lit up the world. When she shook her hair, all my troubles went away. Before I could say anything, she kissed my left cheek and went past me, calling out over her shoulder, "I've got to go to work, and Tony's waiting for you." A welcome kiss. But I had to put her out of my mind.

Tony's door was open, and I saw the stuff he hadn't already taken to Lagunitas packed in an open suitcase. He stood, uneasy in the middle of the room. "Want a chair or a bed?"

"No. You can start your own yard sale."

"You know how close we came to getting popped today? Jack stopped you to talk on the way out. We stopped two or three times in the Panhandle. Nate wanted to talk about a narc trying to buy five thousand. We could easily have been at Blake's when the bust went down."

"But we weren't."

"I can't do it anymore."

"I can't do it without you."

"Fuck. You can if you want. You're good at it. Careful. Cool. Hell, you're a fucking freak's freak." He gave me a big hug, and I hugged him back until I felt a tear run down my cheek. He stepped back and wiped his eyes. "Hell, man. You're crying too."

"I'm not completely Spock."

He took the car to Lagunitas. I wouldn't need it for a few days. Besides, it was half his.

Went up to my flat and tried to shower my feelings away or maybe just my thoughts. Packed my small bag and put on some righteous threads—black leather boots, blue corduroys, a striped shirt, and a leather jacket. Then I realized I was ready early, and Jack wasn't even here.

I flipped through some records in the living room, put on a Richard and Mimi Fariña, and closed my eyes. I was all dressed up on a total downer day—Blake busted, Tony quitting, and I'm listening to an album I completely dig by a guy killed on a motorcycle. When the side finished, I sat in an awful, lonely silence.

Jack interrupted with a nervous smile. "We got to split."

He didn't wait for me, just headed down the stairs. He had the motor going, and after I jumped in, he accelerated up to about forty-five.

"Cool it, Jack. I'm holding the stuff you wanted me to bring."

He throttled back. "Sorry!"

"Where are we going?"

"Russian Hill. Miranda's cousin lent her a house there. The other chick is Veronica. I barely know her. Miranda, I've known since we were born. We've had a thing a few times, but it never lasts. She's complicated and gets bored easy."

"You're telling me it doesn't last because she gets bored? This is Jack talking, right?"

He shrugged. "She's different. She can be really fun, but she always wants things her way."

"You hung up on her? Are you going to flip out if she comes on to me?"

"She'll get what she wants, and there's no use getting upset. I got over that long ago."

My Dick Tracy sexual mystery decoder ring hit the jackpot. Jack was totally hung up on this Miranda but couldn't have her all to himself, so he had to ball everyone else in sight to keep his mind off her.

It never worked that way with me. I never forgot a girl I'd cared for, even if I wanted to.

We pulled into the driveway in front of a two-car garage. I handed him one of the two tins of joints I'd brought. I'd rather not have him looking for me the whole time.

A heavy wooden door set in a stone arch guarded the house. The world stopped as a blond opened it, ignored Jack, weighed me up with green eyes, and filed away her conclusions.

Her eyes still on me, she invited us in, released me from her gaze, and whispered something to Jack that yielded a nervous laugh. He started to whisper back, but she took a step toward me. Her lightly tanned flesh set off against a shimmering dark blue sleeveless dress. There was something athletic about her arms—swimmer, probably. "I'm Miranda." She didn't wait for me to respond. She moved back to Jack, gave him a passing kiss, and led us to the dining room.

The table could have seated eight easily but was set in an odd manner for four with one place at either end and an accompanying place to the right of each end.

"We're going to start dinner. Jack and I have a party we need to make, and I'm on East Coast time." She took one end of the table, with Jack at her side, and didn't need to ask me to take the other end. "Veronica will be down soon. She had a call from her family."

A fiftyish man in black slacks and a crisp white shirt came out of a door near Miranda, poured wine, and disappeared. Miranda and Jack kept at their conversation, and I half thought about leaving until Veronica appeared next to me. She was dressed all in black, save for a red and black patterned scarf.

She grinned beneath calm, blue eyes and held out a Zippo. "Bring any grass?"

I discarded any thought of leaving and produced a joint.

"Give them one, and they'll leave us alone."

"Already gave Jack a tin."

She blew a few smoke rings in my direction before inhaling and passing it my way. The guy reappeared with bowls of soup and eyed the joint. I handed him one, generating a slight bow and an exit toward the kitchen. The soup was just the potato side of creamy, and the wine had an almost licorice flavor.

Miranda seemed to notice everything. She stood up and walked toward us with her glass. "You shouldn't have done that. It might distract them from cooking."

"I'll cut them off until dessert."

She rested her free hand on my shoulder. "Everything all right, Veronica?"

Veronica said, "Just my family." She looked at me and then back at Miranda. "I have to go to Atherton tomorrow."

"Well, I'm taking Jack out tonight. I'm sure you'll get along without us." She pulled her fingertips across my shoulder and walked back to the head of the table with a light rustle of her dress.

I passed the joint back to Veronica and asked, "Your family's here in the Bay Area?"

"An uncle. My father is visiting him with his new bride."

"Do you get along with her?"

"We haven't met, but I'm deathly curious to see if she's older than me." She took a long draw on the joint, released, and asked, "How about yours?"

"I never think of them. One of the advantages of dropping out."

She nodded and switched topics. "You live in the same house with Jack. Do you two go out scouting chicks together?"

"Jack's not really into chicks; he's into balling. Other than Miranda, the chick isn't all that important." That earned a smile.

"And how about you?"

"I'm totally fascinated by women. How they're so different from each other. Personality, desires, ankles, ears, toes, all so different."

"That's an odd collection of body parts."

"Just examples." Time to change the subject. "Do you travel with Miranda?"

"No, we're old friends, but—" She paused. "We're *different*." She tasted the wine, and the guy wearing black and white brought out the main course: dumplings in a white sauce.

"Why'd you come this time?"

"I wanted to get out of my shell and create some memories."

"Would I need a crab cracker or just a little oyster knife?"

"Who's to say I need help? Or that it would be you, if I did?"

"Good questions." I tried the dumplings—chewy with hints of fish, cream, and wine from the sauce. "These are tasty. What are they?"

"They're made from pike, Quenelles de Brochet." She wasn't trying to be superior with her French, just matter of fact. "Miranda loves them. Do you speak any French?"

"Just a little backyard Spanish and three years of high school German."

"Why'd you pick that? Everybody takes French or Italian."

"I don't know. Maybe because I was reading *All Quiet on the Western Front* when it was time to pick a language." I asked, "And you? French or Italian?"

"What?"

"You said everyone took French or Italian…"

"French. French history major." She took some water and leaned toward me. "Miranda told me you're a big dealer."

"Just a little cog in the wheel of psychedelic distribution."

"Modesty can be attractive, obfuscation less so."

"What do you want to know?"

"All about it. I want to know about something…out of the ordinary."

I gave her the long version, which intrigued her but didn't keep her from retreating to her room without dessert. I savored a chocolate mousse and hit the library. Perused books on Oceanic art and lost myself for a while reading about these wonderful instruments from the island of Truk—love sticks they were called. Thought about leaving again but trudged up the stairs to my assigned room. At the landing, I couldn't ignore a colorful trail laid out on the hardwood floor. I wasn't good at naming colors, but there was butterscotch, an extraordinarily bright red, some kind of purple, and a navy polka dot. Colorful panties placed in a winding curve, taking my eyes past a closed door and ending with a maroon pair in front of a slightly ajar door.

Such an invitation begged a response. I slipped the panties over my head, arranging them into a many-hued garland. Opened the door. There was Veronica, barely under the covers. She laughed and laughed. "Get those off, you freak!"

I kneeled next to the bed. "I return them safely to my Lady Veronica."

She removed them and tugged me into the bed, but I stopped almost as soon as we started. "What's going on?" She reasonably wanted to know.

"You said you came with Miranda to do wild things and create extraordinary memories."

"I'm listening."

"Your panties gave me the idea. You arranged them in curves."

"The curves of a woman, in case you didn't get the idea."

"Lombard Street is a big tourist attraction because of its curves. It's close to here." I kissed her forehead but knew I'd have to stop that or I'd never make it to Lombard.

"Go on."

"We could fuck on it from top to bottom on one side and up the other—kind of like the twelve Stations of the Cross."

She hopped out of bed, assessed her clothes in the closet, and put on a pleated skirt, a big black sweater, and a knit cap. With sex suspended and anticipated, we ventured into the dark, cool night, striding and holding hands out along Leavenworth.

At the base of Lombard Street, we sat on a step on the left side, making out like high schoolers. We stood next to a garage door and groped all over for the second station. Headlights glanced around the fog as we moved up to station three for tongue trading. A low wall was our fourth stop. She sat on my lap, and I raised her sweater to pay attention to her breasts—kissing, nibbling, and fondling. In a doorway alcove, I entered the gates of heaven. She braced herself, and we found a rhythm. Quivering, we broke apart and heard a cable car approaching above. She ran for it, and I followed, marveling at her. At the end of the line, we started toward the Buena Vista Café, but behind the big windows, it was crowded with noisy gestures and too many straights.

We walked away from the café and toward the bay. Veronica took in the briny scent of the bay and quickened her pace, stopping only to strip. I didn't want to do it, but I was too much of a chicken to look like a coward and followed her into the shallow water. She whooped around, while I was too cold to do anything but shiver. She walked out in triumph, shaking water off like a flapping seal. I let her use my T-shirt to dry off. Not exactly Sir Walter Raleigh.

"We've got to get warm. I know a restaurant nearby."

Freaks weren't all that welcome on the wharf. We could scare away the tourists. A couple of us, though, had nurtured Sclioto's. We'd show up late in the evening when it was quiet and tip well. Even so, Veronica and I could be pushing our luck tonight, but we hustled into the restrooms and reappeared looking presentable enough. They put us in a c-shaped booth to either hide us, celebrate our transformation, or possibly because the place was almost empty.

Troy, our cultivated waiter, earned his tip by bringing unordered hot tea with the menus. We ordered two bowls of cioppino and slid up next to each other in the middle of the booth.

"Have you done that with any other girl?"

"What? Jump in nearly freezing water?"

"No, the Stations of the Cross."

"No, and I'm saving the last six for you."

That earned a kiss and a wandering hand.

Two steaming bowls came, and we happily worked at the stew—cracking crab, shelling shrimp, and warming our bodies with fish flesh and tomato broth. We followed the stew with a bowl of warm rice pudding and two spoons.

I wanted us to save our remaining energy and suggested, "We should get a cab back."

She looked around the empty restaurant and back to me. "To the top of that crooked street?"

Was she serious? "I have visions of a warm bed."

***

I woke alone to a tray with rolls and juice on the nightstand next to me. I ate and threw open the curtains to what must have been early evening. Went out into the hall and found my cure-all: a bathroom with an enclosed shower. It let loose a powerful gush that reminded me of the communal blockhouse showers at the Oasis for Mobile Living.

Refreshed, I dressed in leather pants and a western shirt and went looking for the others. Only Miranda was there, cross-legged on the couch in tight red pedal pushers, a half-buttoned white silk blouse, and a ruby dangling above her breasts. "Veronica enjoyed herself last night," she said.

I sat on the other end of the couch, lit a joint, and handed it to her. "Is this kiss-and-tell?"

"No need. I have a good imagination." She took her time with the joint but eventually passed it back. "I'm afraid we're all alone for at least a day or two. If you're up for it, that is?"

"I'm sure we could find plenty to read in the library."

"You couldn't find what I want there."

"What's that?"

"Smack." Her eyes studied my surprise. "You haven't done it before?"

"No!"

"Most people can't handle it. You have to be able to stop on a dime." She drilled me with her half smile. "I just like it to party with a man. I didn't want it with Jack, but I want it with you."

She was playing me, but it had a certain enchantment. "Why?"

"It slows everything down and stretches it all out." Her green eyes held me again, inviting and commanding me.

I wondered aloud. "You have a connection here?"

"Jack tells me you know all about these things." She stretched a leg out on the couch, tickling my chest with bright blue, polished toenails. "Don't you know about these things?"

"Don't know anybody dealing smack and can't go around asking. I don't need the gossip."

Her lips moved but not for words, just to remind me she was waiting. Her blouse was now open. Moments before, I couldn't have ever imagined agreeing to this, but now with her painted toes resting against my chest, I thought maybe I could cross this line and slip right back. Tony could slip out of his careful self now and then. Why couldn't I? And so not too reluctantly, I had an idea. "Near the Fillmore, there's a drive-in we go to after concerts for sweet potato pie. They have other things there, but I love the sweet potato pie. There's usually a bunch of cats standing around the cars. Always assumed they were dealing smack."

She pulled her leg back, leaned over, and kissed me before standing up. "Let's go."

She reminded me of Mother, so out front sexually. I didn't know whether I wanted to scream or go.

She buttoned up her blouse. "C'mon. We can fuck for days, but let's get the smack."

"Okay, but let's dress more subdued." I changed into jeans, a work shirt, Keds, and a blue plaid jacket. She put on her dope-scoring outfit—jeans, a dark sweater, and a gray army surplus coat.

"I came in Jack's car. Do you have one?" I asked.

"We can use what's in the garage."

There were two. The least conspicuous was a white Jaguar sedan.

"Do you have a driver's license?"

"Yes. Don't you want to drive me?"

I took the registration out of the glove box. "Who's this?"

"My cousin."

"Good. You drive."

The drive-in sat in the middle of a parking area with white walls, chest to ceiling glass, and a wraparound, upward-tilting awning like the hat on the Statue of Liberty. The awning caught and reflected all the neon light. I'd come here after smoking pot many times, but I didn't think I could manage the place on acid or psilocybin. The bouncing, reverberating white light would send me reeling. We parked, and she looked surprised. "Everyone here's Black!"

"I guess you don't get sweet potato pie." I opened the door. "Watch me and stay in the car."

I ordered the pie and added fried prawns to buy some time. Moved away from the register and leaned back against the counter on the side closest to the cats that interested me. Took out a joint and twiddled it in the fingers of my right hand, so they could see, but I made sure it was hidden from the inside of the drive-in.

Didn't take long for a cat to come up, light jumping off his open white shirt with long collar points. He leaned back onto the counter next to me. "What're you looking for?"

I cupped the joint in my hand and dropped it in his. "Dime bags. Four."

He didn't respond at first, perhaps waiting for some signal I didn't pick up on. After a sign from someone or maybe just after reflecting, he said, "Over there with the hat like mine, leaning against the Chevy."

My order was ready, and I took it over to the Chevy.

Cat with the hat said, "You some ballsy ass motherfucker coming in here like that!"

"I had to fit in somehow, and I'm sort of white." That didn't score a direct hit on his funny bone, but he had a hint of a smile.

"What do you want, sort of whitey?"

"Four dime bags."

I offered him a prawn, but he wasn't interested.

"What's in the other bag?"

"Sweet potato pie."

"Drop the money in there."

Damn. I wanted the pie, but I gave it to him.

He dropped four tied-up balloons in my jacket pocket. "You don't look like no strung-out junkie, and this stuff ain't been stepped on much. You get me?"

"How much for a hit?"

"A quarter. Maybe a third." I started to go, but he stopped me. "Got any more weed?"

"Sorry, man."

"You come again, bring a few sticks."

I nodded and left with the smack and my unwanted fried prawns.

Miranda didn't like the smell of the prawns, but I didn't want to litter and needed distance from the drive-in, so I opened a window. We turned up Clay, and I had her stop at Webster, where I'd spotted a trash bin. I got out and dumped the prawns. There was a hospital up the street, and I liked the look of the buildings with their clean proportions and spare details. Victorians could be too elaborate. I wondered what it was like to be an architect.

Miranda called to me, "Mark, we don't need a hospital."

I hopped back in. "Sorry. That building was kind of cool."

"Jack told me you were super careful, and you're dawdling with smack in your pocket…"

I kissed her shoulder as she drove off. "If a cop comes, I say, 'Sorry, Officer. My mother passed away up there. Sometimes I stand here and think of her.' He'd apologize and leave."

She flashed a smirk that said, "You got me but I'm not admitting it."

We parked the car, and I followed her into her bedroom. Three walls were the color of jeans you'd gotten used to. Darker blue curtains kept the world away on the other wall. I took one of the armchairs flanking a small, round table and watched her gather equipment. Out of a large suitcase came a Red Cross bag with syringes, saline vials, gauze, and tape. From a smaller case, she took an antique spoon, and from her purse, she took an industrial strength lighter. She laid it all out on the table next to me and said, "You haven't done this before?"

"No." And now that it was here in front of me, did I really want to?

She worked in a blur. I was completely captivated. She was in charge, efficient and sure of what she was doing— opening the balloon, pouring, mixing, heating, and drawing it into the syringe. "I'll do you first. Pump your fist." She was so quick with it all, tying my bicep with something silk and running her fingers along my forearm. "You're a virgin. These veins are magnificent." She looked into my eyes. "You watching or looking away, stud?"

I watched. She guided the needle in. My blood billowed into the syringe chamber in pulsing red ribbons. Without wasted motion, she plunged the smack in and pulled the syringe. Caught me in the back of the throat, warm fuzzies spread up my shoulders, through my head, and down my thighs. I stretched out, wrapped tight in a long cocoon.

"Hold this." She placed my hand on the spot where she'd injected me. She sat back on the other side of the table, mixed another fix, injected it into her foot, and sprawled back—her expression somewhere between serene and dead.

My mind came and went, eyelids beyond my control.

"What was his name?" she slurred.

"Whose name?"

"The dealer."

"Ray…Raymond."

"Fucker was right… Hadn't been stepped on. Almost pure…"

Wished she were quiet.

"Won't need all those bags. It's so fucking good. Could snort it."

I'll just let her not be there. Fuck time. Fuck hours. Fuck minutes. Nice cocoon. Nice warm cocoon. Drifting…

Raised my head, looking around. Her head sagged, chin bobbing.

She held her hand out like a Don't Walk sign. I wasn't walking anywhere. Warm and slow. Slow. Warm and slow. Going nowhere.

Watched her smile. Watched her get out of the chair. Watched her kneel between my legs. My eyes blinked. Rested her head on my thigh. Her hand caressed my crotch. My eyes stayed open. I went along on her smack lover's tour of the *Kama Sutra*; her favorite had me imitating a sawhorse while she did her best cowgirl.

***

Next day, we cabbed downtown, so she could visit a banker. I waited outside, leaning against a wall and trying to piece together the previous night. I'd lost control. Totally exquisite but I'd let her take over. When had I last let a chick take over? Long time.

Twice, I was bolted from my thoughts by straights trying to score weed. And damn, they only wanted a couple of joints. I sent them on their way, doing my best to look offended, but the heat showed up, two of them.

"What are you doing here?"

"Officers, I'm just waiting for my girlfriend, and twice businessmen have tried to buy drugs." I gave them my pure look. "What is it, officers? The hair? Gee, you need some hair for the girls."

"Mark!" My personal cavalry arrived in the earthly form of Miranda wearing a tight red skirt made from bullfighter capes. She shook her hair as she put on big, round sunglasses. Jesus, she could give a blind eunuch a hard-on, and the cops weren't blind.

"Officers, my boyfriend may look mischievous, but he really is an angel."

I swear they were about to doff their hats to her.

She asked, "My banker suggested a seafood restaurant on Bush. Could you point us?"

The cop with the most stripes pointed up the street. "Go up to Montgomery. Then left two blocks to Bush. Turn right, and you'll see it on your right, just before Kearny."

"Thank you, Officer." She took my arm, and we walked off toward lunch as she worked wonders with the bullfighter capes. The heat lost all interest in me.

Someday, I'd figure out why the banks on this street had so many columns or what columns had to do with money. Big ones, Greek or Roman. I didn't know. Lots of columns on the right side, fluted with scrolls on the top. Fluted and unfluted on the left, both with scrolls on the top. Didn't Jesus throw the moneylenders out of the temple?

We turned onto Montgomery, and I said, "This is where a lot of the guys pay protection money."

"Protection?"

"Retainers. Lots of lawyers here and some of the guys pay to have one ready."

"Do you?"

"No. Thought about it. I know who to call. But I decided if I had a lawyer, it would remove all doubt from the cops if they popped me. A lot of busts are just being at the wrong place at the wrong time. You're in a car or a house, and somebody else is holding. So, I thought that not having a lawyer right away might look better. I could have it all wrong, but that's my thinking."

We saw the restaurant on an alley before Kearny. Sam's, it was. They put us in number fourteen—a curtained booth with rickety chairs, a white tablecloth on a narrow table, sliced lemons, sourdough bread, and a buzzer.

Miranda charmed the crust off the waiter, and when she shook her shoulders, she removed any thought he'd had of carding us. He came back with a dry white in an ice bucket, and they negotiated a menu of dishes to share: salad with shellfish, boned sand dabs, fried zucchini, and crepes with anisette. He closed the curtains and left with a light step.

She ignored the wine and sipped water. "Why'd you handle the drive-in that way?"

The shot of smack was long gone. I sipped the wine. "There weren't any white people for blocks, and Black cops hardly exist around here. The cats there would have spotted them anyway. The problem was that they might've been worried about us. Twiddling the joint solved that."

The waiter placed the salad between us, and we leaned into it. The shellfish was fresh crab and bay shrimp. The tangy oil and vinegar kick-started my taste buds.

Miranda asked, "Ever been to the Union Oyster Bar at Grand Central?"

"When I was young, my grandfather took me. I loved it. Shrimp cocktails. Crab cakes." I could see him sitting next to me—suit and a snappy tie, serious eyes, but always a smile for me.

"I sit at the counter by myself, eating oysters and watching men." She sank her teeth into a crab leg. If being thin was the current trend for women, Miranda didn't give a damn. She enjoyed maintaining her curves and sure wasn't on a brown rice diet. "I like to watch them react to me. Most are obvious—heads turning and big eye movements. I study the ones with calm eyes." She pulled off a chunk of sourdough and buttered it. "So, why are you so calm?"

"I'm sitting with a beautiful woman and starting a meal. Why shouldn't I be calm?"

"Don't I shock you?" She was trying to, but she was nowhere close.

"Not yet."

The main course arrived—sand dabs with a touch of sweetness and zucchini with just a little crunch. Great contrast.

She raised her wine glass. "You're not daring me. You just don't want to answer the question."

"I've had extensive training."

"By whom?"

What the hell. "Let's say for the sake of argument that you had a kid, and your family or trusts cut off the money. That kid would be me."

As the waiter set down the crepes with anisette, she startled him with a sharp laugh, but he recuperated and left. The crepes were chewy and warm, and the sauce was hot with a hint of licorice.

"That explains things," she said. And then, with a shocking lack of further interest in the subject, she said, "I've never been to San Francisco before. Take me someplace interesting."

"What have you seen so far?"

"The airport, a party in Sea Cliff last night, and the bank this morning."

I knew a sight for this chick. "Are you a runner or a swimmer?"

"Swimmer. Why?"

"Just checking to see if you're in shape enough for a walk."

We cabbed back to her place to change shoes and find a map to orient myself. I couldn't figure out how to get her there and also be certain of maintaining the surprise. There were too many hills along the way. I'd have to think on my feet and keep to lower ground as best as I could.

There were a few awkward moments, but I improvised, pointing out other sights and giving impromptu kisses. In North Beach, I maneuvered her into Washington Square Park across from Saints Peter and Paul, and there it was on top of Telegraph Hill—Coit Tower, two hundred feet tall, erect, and spewing fog.

"You delicious bastard. You brought me here to see a giant prick on top of a hill."

"No," I protested. "I wanted to show you the murals inside."

"No, you didn't." She wasn't the type to cuff me on the shoulder. She just found a bench in the park from which to admire the tower.

With her touring needs fulfilled, we went back to her borrowed place and stood in the kitchen, drinking ice water and passing a joint. She exhaled just to the side of me. "I don't want to bring out the smack today. I never do it two days in a row."

She didn't explain, but it was an easy guess. Smack had a terrible reputation for a good reason, and she wouldn't tolerate losing control. I could do without it. It deadened my only real asset—my brain. As for all the fucking, I was sure I'd have enjoyed it more if I was sober. I couldn't resist playing with her though. "Any other limits on our activities?"

She looked at my belt—smooth brown leather with a double ring buckle—uncinched it, and pulled it off one pant loop at a time. "No. Do you need any?"

***

We were hungry for dinner by seven and ordered from a Chinese delivery place. We sat at the big mahogany dining table, eating out of the delivery cartons.

"You know, you fuck like a Jewish guy."

"No, I fuck like myself."

"You're so free with your body." She poured more wine. "How did you get so wild and free?"

Wild and free maybe but I was dead certain that the only time I let my guard down—the only time I wasn't on the lookout for danger—was in bed with a woman, and I just wanted to make the time last and last. But this was Miranda, and she had to be fended off. She was over the top exciting all right, but this chick was not safe. "I wasn't till I met you."

"Bullshit!"

She continued her ethnic tour. "Did you ever do it with a Black?"

"No." A defect in my belief in racial equality.

"Would you?"

"Sure, but I don't meet any Black chicks. I have a Black friend, but he moved to Colorado. Black chicks, though, I just don't meet any."

Her eyes and face were doing the speaking now, and I had trouble understanding.

"You know what I want."

Lord, I was dense. My time was up, and she wanted a Black.

"Why be a prude? Jack brought you here."

"It seems sudden."

"There'll be another time."

Maybe. Maybe not. "Who's the lucky guy?"

"That guy from the other night. Raymond, wasn't it?"

"You only saw him from ten yards or so. What if he talks with a squeaky voice?"

"I can read men, and ten yards is enough." She studied me for a moment. "You ready to go?"

"What do you need me for?"

"I don't know exactly where it is, and I've been thinking it through. I don't know how I'd manage it. You, though, could get him in the car."

It was too early in the day to go to the drive-in. The dealers wouldn't be there until dark. So, I put on my best reflective look and pushed back my chair. She didn't waste time, stood up, and walked behind me, musk and sandalwood wafting. Ran her fingers through my hair. "You know, I can convince you."

"Convince me."

***

The Jaguar had less than a quarter tank. She didn't want to fill it up, but near empty tanks made me nervous, so she stopped at a station.

"We had plenty of gas."

"Could be an earthquake."

That started her laughing. Big Brother came on the radio playing "Combination of the Two." We got into the beat until a commercial came, and I turned it off. She parked right next to the walk-up counter, just as she had before.

Raymond leaned against a Buick, but first, I was going to get the sweet potato pie I'd lost out on last time. I carried the bag over to Raymond.

He looked me up and down. "How many?"

"Different subject." That merited an inquisitive look. "The chick in the car behind me. She's the subject."

His eyes widened. "You her pimp?"

No need to get offended. "Call it a matchmaker."

"Trouble satisfying her?"

"I put in my shift."

"And she wants some dark meat?"

This was taking a predictable wrong turn. "I'm just a messenger." I focused on his eyes. "She is one hell of a woman."

"She does look that." He turned his head, searching for somebody, maybe a partner. "I got to leave something with my man over there. I'll be with you."

I sat in the back of the car. When he got in the front, I introduced him. "Raymond, this is Miranda. Miranda, Raymond."

Back at the house, they went to Miranda's blue room, while I went to the kitchen. Then, while carrying a glass of water upstairs, I had visions of colorful panties, but all I found was a note from Veronica.

Mark, I thought it would be special with you, but I saw you with Miranda, and it was too much for me.

Jesus. What had she expected?

Losing my touch

Next day, I was sitting on my building steps, avoiding a decision I had to make. Would I keep the business up? Didn't want a new partner and working by myself was too risky. Did I want to go to college? Could I get into a good one? I wasn't really thinking about my future though. I was mostly watching cars and pedestrians go by.

Marie came walking toward me, carrying groceries. If I'd had an older sister, it would've been her. She taught me cooking, remedial social niceties, and just big sister kind of stuff. I relieved her of the bags and lugged them into the kitchen, for which I got a peck. She took off her big jacket, uncovering a blue turtleneck and a maroon necklace, probably one she'd made.

"Hungry?" she asked. "I'm making a tomato and zucchini gratin."

"I'll help."

She sharpened up our one chef's knife before showing me the angle she wanted the vegetables cut.

"What's up with Jack?" She lit a joint. "Weren't you with him somewhere? He came back here all uptight and left in a big hurry."

"Not sure." What could I say? I could give her my theory but couldn't do it without descending into kiss-and-tell.

She laughed at my reluctance. "You know, Mark, everyone around here talks about everyone else's love life, shacking up and balling. You're about the only one who doesn't join in."

"Is that true?" God, did we have to do this?

After I sliced the zucchinis on the diagonal and the tomatoes into rounds, she had me grate cheese. "You're not dense, Mark. Don't you listen when people talk?"

"Course I listen to gossip. I just don't pay attention when it gets down to who's slipping out the back door and who's two-timing. I figure I don't want people to talk about me, so I don't talk about them."

"Are you actually freaking serious? People talk about you all the time!" Her voice was raised slightly, but she put the gratin in the oven without a sound.

"Oh, what do they say?" Why did I ask? Talking with women was often a slippery slope.

She sat across from me, full head of long brown hair thrown high and back off her face. "Tell me about Jack first."

We'd finished the joint, and I said, "Open a bottle of Jack's wine, and I'll think about it."

She put her hands on her hips and asked, "Why don't you open one?"

"You know which one will go best."

"I'll pick, and you open."

She took the gratin out of the oven, spread cheese on top, and put it back in. Then she brought me a bottle with a label in Italian.

I pulled the cork and asked, "Why'd you pick this one?" I didn't want to talk about Jack and didn't really need to hear what people thought of me.

"It's red, it's Italian, and I'm cooking something with tomatoes. Now, tell me about Jack."

The oven had warmed the room, and she took off her sweater, leaving a plain white T-shirt, nipples showing, maroon necklace dangling. She drew her hands through her hair and shook it out, releasing such an agreeable waft of lavender that I gave in. Gave in because I'd laughed a lot with her over the months in the flat; gave in because it was warm in the kitchen with aromas of tomatoes; gave in because she was sort of a big sister, sometimes a bossy big sister; and gave in because I had a joint and a glass of wine in front of me.

"Jack's totally hung up on a chick he grew up with back East. I mean, totally lost-his-mind hung up. They've had a thing now and then, but she's really not into him, and she uses him. But he's semi-blind to all that and thinks he can have her."

"You met her?"

"Yeah, she was here with a friend of hers, and Jack invited me to party with them."

"And he got upset because she ditched him for you. But you wouldn't have gone for it if he were there. So, let me guess. He leaves, the other girl disappears, and you're alone with her."

"You could be a detective, specializing in love. But the other girl didn't disappear. She had to visit family."

"Same difference." She set the gratin on the table, and I spooned it out between us. She usually made this with potatoes instead of zucchini, but this was just as good. "Tell me about Jack's girl. What's her name?"

"Miranda. A very complicated chick. She arranges other people's lives to get what she wants."

"So, Jack's a piece of furniture."

"Basically."

Marie paused with a forkful of zucchini suspended in the air, waiting for me to continue.

"Detective Marie has probably already figured this out, but Jack's on a mission to ball every chick on the planet. It's the only way he can keep his mind off Miranda."

She swirled the wine in the quarter-filled glass but set it down without taking a sip. "So, you ended up as part of the furniture, too?"

"A comfortable armchair."

"It's good for you to be tossed now and then. Keep that ego in check."

"It's checked regularly."

"You know, a lot of chicks think you're uptight and that you don't like them because they're too fat, too skinny, or too this or that."

The problem was that whenever I got to talking with a chick—really talking, emotional stuff—it was hard to stop. "Like who?"

"Lots! Remember Carla?" She lit the joint back up for the last few tokes.

"What about Carla?" Hadn't seen her in a long time but I thought we were friends.

"She invited you to her room at that flat on Haight just above Divisadero. She wanted you, but you spent hours talking about an old girlfriend. Finally, you just left, and she went out and found the first cat that interested her."

"Yeah, I couldn't get a girl off my mind that night."

Before I could say anything else, she went on. "Okay, tell me about when it didn't work for you. Give me one." She filled my glass.

All that came to mind was Charlotte. Charlotte downstairs. She'd invited me to see her room after I'd painted it, and she'd finished decorating. We smoked some weed and stretched out on her bed, relaxing. Without me initiating anything at all, she unbuttoned her dress and slid next to me. I tried because she'd wanted it, but I was all a mess. Kissing her too hard and too fast. The posters on the wall of large women drinking champagne, and with Charlotte herself being on the plus side, it broke out memories of that large Florida bitch raping scrawny fourteen-year-old me.

When my heart raced, and I pulled away, Charlotte freaked, thinking it was about her. I couldn't let her think that, though, so I told her all about it. We talked for hours and fell asleep together. But I couldn't tell any of this to Marie.

"C'mon, Mark. I'm waiting!"

"All right but only one."

"There was only one, or you're only going to tell me one?"

I ignored her question "All right. Tony and I picked up two college chicks, the first or second time we took any to Lagunitas. I walked out in the forest with the dark-haired one. She was cool, and we sat next to each other in this open area, looking up at the sky. I turned to her as she pulled back her hair, and her profile was virtually identical to this chick in Tucson who'd done me wrong. It just froze me and flushed any desire. She must've thought I was a complete idiot."

Marie got up, poured a glass of ice water, and sipped, leaning against the refrigerator. "One thing's for sure. No other guy I've met would tell me a story like that and sit there, head up, untroubled."

What was I supposed to say to that?

She put the glass down on top of the refrigerator and ran her hands through her hair again. This time, she sent it up from the right side and let it cascade down the left side of her head. "What do you think about my hair when it's this way?"

Good. A different topic. "It's wild. Distinctive and different from other chicks."

"What do you think about me?"

Holy shit, Batman. This wasn't true confessions anymore. No more big sister. Had to take a sip of wine just to pause and collect myself. I'd never thought of Marie that way. "When I moved in here, I was in awe of you. You were so assured, and I was so new. You were out of my reach. I always thought of you as the chick I couldn't touch."

"But you're wrong." She tossed me her T-shirt. "I'm quite touchable."

∗∗∗

Next morning, Marie split early to show her jewelry someplace, and she left without asking if I'd be here tonight, but she never had asked before. I just felt crummy and alone. Last night meant nothing. I went into my room, but it gave me no relief. It was so Spartan, so clean, and so organized. It forced my thoughts toward decisiveness. But I just didn't feel like deciding anything. Tony called to tell me he was coming down to pick me up, so we could talk and settle up. Total bummer. There was no use in trying to talk him out of it. Had to get used to having no partner, no sidekick, and no more adventures with Tony Patchouli.

I put a jacket on to go outside and found one of the dime bags I'd gotten from Raymond in a pocket. Fucking careless. I'm losing my touch. Having a damn balloon in my jacket and not even knowing it was there! How stupid! Anyway, hadn't I given them all to Miranda? Totally confusing. What do I do with it? Keep it? For what? I put it in my hollowed-out book for now.

Decided to walk up to the street to see somebody, anybody I knew. Had to get rid of this rotten feeling. Put on a hat that I'd bought who knows when but had never worn. It was a kind of rustic Panama. Outside, there was nothing new to report, just wind and fog. The hat kept threatening to ride the breeze in the Panhandle, but it behaved in the lee of the buildings on the other side.

The street was crowded with unfamiliar faces. Gust of wind took the hat. I caught it, but the same thing happened again, and I dumped it in the nearest trash can. Bought a piroshky and ate it while standing outside. A tour bus went by, cameras clicking. Wished I had my hat for a real flourish but still performed a couple of sweeping sarcastic bows for the cameras.

Started walking down the street and some cat I'd never seen was wearing my hat. Pissed me off, so I retrieved it from his head and smashed it into a different trash can. People froze and stared. The cat stood, stuck there with his mouth wide open.

I gave him a piece of my mind. "I put that hat in the trash because I didn't like it. I don't want anybody else wearing it."

Could hear myself yelling. Idiot! What the hell was I doing? Not low profile and I was being an asshole on top of it.

Nothing but frowns and shaking heads to be seen until old Karl came up to the newly hatless one. "Sorry, man. He's a good cat. He just had a bad trip."

Karl steered me away. "What the fuck is with you? It's just a hat, you stupid shit." Wasn't much to do or say when someone was reading it to you and they were right. "Fuck it! C'mon with me."

A few blocks away, Jed let us into his flat with a shaky hand, his long black hair falling like medieval armor around his head. The living room was strewn with freaks. I sat next to Karl on the floor. Joints moved clockwise and counter, and stories went in all directions. Cat from New York had agreed on a price and came in to pick up four keys. When Jamie got to his hotel with the keys, the fucking sleaze lowered his price, and Jamie was stuck either leaving with the keys or hardly making anything on the deal. Jed saw Annette Funicello walking down the street, wearing Mickey Mouse ears for her top. Everybody wanted a picture. Nate said some dude had come into town, talking up his weed, and the samples from the open brick were good, but the bricks he sold were crap. Frank said he had to leave the Haight because he was tired of girls with hairy legs, but he was afraid he'd forgotten how to unhook a bra. Most of the stories I didn't hear since I was preoccupied with being pissed at myself. I needed to confess but where? I thanked Karl for the rescue and left Jed's place in search of relief. In the Panhandle, three chicks were twirling, playing a flute, and blowing bubbles. Way too joyful for me.

Tony came, and I banged my fingers putting a suitcase full of clothes and books into the trunk of the Olds.

He asked, "How'd that party with Jack go?"

"Long story, man. Can we leave it for another time? I'm bummed out."

"About what?"

"Caused a scene on the street. Jammed that Panama hat in the trash and found a cat wearing it, so I ripped it off his head. Karl rescued me."

"Did you hit the cat?" Tony asked.

"No. Felt like it, though!" And that was the fucking worst. I had felt like hitting him.

"You're going to need all that good karma you've built up if you do more shit like that."

"I know. And it was over nothing. If I lose it over nothing, I could lose it at the wrong time."

I wished he'd say something. Tell me off. Tell me what to do. I was tired of being alone. But he was silent as we left the city. Silent until we were over the bridge. Not until we were in the first tunnel did he spill what was on his mind.

"I went to the Russian River, to Carlos and Annie's, and saw those two chicks. Remember Wendy and Dawn? The ones we rescued?"

The thought of them revived me. "Totally. What's up with them?"

"They're the only ones there that know anything about farming or cooking. They're doing fine and will probably be running the place soon—as much as anybody does."

"Did they remember you?"

He grinned. "Absolutely. They'd love to see you."

"Soon. Soon, maybe."

Then he laid it on me. "I'm leaving Lagunitas and moving up there."

Now the day was really bringing me down.

"Mark, I really dug all the shit we did, but I need a change. Maybe you do, too. Losing it on the street isn't a good sign."

"Maybe. Right now, I just feel like crap, so can we just turn up the radio and let me tune out till we get home?"

At the lodge, we collected our stashes from the woods and from the hideaway Tony had built under the deck. We dumped the cash and an assortment of weed, mescaline, acid, hash, and psilocybin onto my bed in the cabin. Twenty thousand in cash wasn't a lot for all those months, but we hadn't been greedy and had given a lot away. We split the money in half and divided the inventory to our own tastes.

Last, we had to decide what to do with the car. Tony said, "It's yours, man. I don't want it up there. Too fancy. Truck or something else low maintenance fits better. I know we used my connections at first, but you always did the Berkeley runs. Take it. It's only fair."

"Maybe I'm giving up the business too. People all around are going back to school. This professor I met at a party said my ACTs are so good that I don't need the high school diploma."

"Trade the Olds in then. It'd pay for most of a used truck. And it's in your name."

"Let me think about it."

We went inside and ate our standard brown rice and squash with Rachel, Danny, and a chick named Chloe who I'd seen around for a few months in the city. She was my age but angelic, not a blemish on her soft skin and just enough fullness in her face. She was taking Tony's old room for a while. She and I had clicked before, but nothing had happened for one reason or another. I was still bummed and needed something to pick me up, so I invited her out to Drakes Beach the next day. She gave me a maybe, which likely meant yes.

In the morning, Tony and I went to the San Rafael car dealers. We found a couple salesmen who hadn't had coffee yet to jolt them out of their hangovers. They thought they could negotiate, but Tony and I were more experienced than they expected, and we got a good deal on a nice-looking Chevy.

Chloe smiled and leaned off the deck as I drove back up to the lodge. I'd forgotten all about her. Couldn't now though. That young female glow. Nipples showing under a sleeveless T-shirt and a tie-dyed skirt waving as she came down the steps.

"I made a picnic for us." She smelled of weed but didn't offer any. That wasn't unusual though; people could think you were already high.

Off we went through the forest, over the hills and onto the peninsula. Drake's Beach had only two cars in the parking lot, and we didn't have to walk far to find a spot all to ourselves in the shelter of the tall cliffs, soft waves rolling in front of us.

She beamed at me. "My sisters and I used to build castles, collect shells, and run in the waves."

"Want to do some collecting?"

"This is probably goofy, but I just want to sit and take it all in."

"Totally cool with me." I spread the blanket out, and we sat close. She with her knees up, arms folded over, and easy all around.

What was I doing here, though? The beach was relaxing, and I could sit here for hours. But why Chloe? I didn't need more chicks. I needed to make a decision.

"You know people in the Haight talk about you." She didn't turn toward me when she spoke.

"What do they say?"

"That you're too intense, and you don't like a lot of people."

This again. "That's pretty heavy. What do you think?"

She nuzzled up. "I get a nice vibe from you, but you don't smile much."

I put on my best smile. "I guess I am intense. I'm almost always thinking about something, always looking for danger, but I was relaxed and smiling a few minutes ago."

"What happened?"

"You told me I was intense and didn't like people."

She put on a pout. "You're playing with me."

"See, I can. I'm not always intense." Now, I really was smiling.

She stood and ran west toward China, calling back at me. "Catch me if you can."

She was fast, but I was still a runner. Thought about tackling her but there was too much driftwood. I put on a burst of speed and got in front of her, cradled her, and twirled her around until she radiated all was well in the world.

We sat, happily entwined, kissing, and rubbing until she pulled back and said, "Balling on the beach can be a bummer. Let's wait till we're back at the lodge."

We delayed at our blanket, eating cheese and tomato sandwiches. Loaded up the Olds and drove out of Drake's Beach. She reclined in her seat, and tilted her head toward me. "Have you done all of the drugs?"

If you'd been around a while, people always asked that. "All the psychedelics."

Gee, she wanted a full inventory. "How about the uppers?"

"I took Dexedrine once and did coke a few times. But it's all bad for me. My mind's naturally going. Add some speed, even a little, makes for a bad scene."

"Any downers?"

"I did smack once."

"Just once?"

"Yeah, just once."

"What was it like?" She rested her left hand on my thigh.

We left the coastal hills and entered the forest. I had to focus on the winding road, but my brain was full of Miranda. Miranda injecting me and then herself. Brain shut off.

Chloe's fingers scratched my thigh as we pulled up in front of the lodge. "What was it like?"

"Everything became warm and cozy very fast. My mind just shut down. I didn't like that, but the chick I did it with liked to ball on it."

"I want to try it."

"I still have some." Shit. I said that without even thinking.

Her face lit up. "Let's do it."

I didn't know why I agreed. Was it her alluring freshness? Was I burned-out on caution? Or was I just ready for anything to divert me from making a decision?

She wanted to go to her room, the one right next to Danny and Rachel's. I got the balloon from my cabin and went back into the lodge and upstairs. She'd decorated her room with colored beads, collages, and tapestries. I moved a teddy bear and sat on a chair next to her bed. She must have snorted coke before because she was prepared, sitting on her bed with an elaborately framed little mirror on her lap. I dumped half of the balloon onto the mirror. She chopped it up a bit, rolled up a dollar bill and took about half of what was on the mirror. I grabbed the mirror as she eased back onto the pillows at the head of her bed.

I watched her breathe before snorting the rest on the mirror. Didn't hit me like before, just creeped up on me. Warm fuzzies and hardly a brain. Happy to have the chair with my feet on the floor but kept losing my eyes, eyelids shutting all by themselves. My head kept snapping up. Maybe I wanted to watch her, but it would drop again, eyes closing. Began to keep my head up, eyes barely open, eyes on Chloe. Miranda and I had fucked for an unrecoverable amount of time. That wasn't happening here, for there was no changing it. Chloe had zoned right out—angelic, asleep, and snoring. I took her shoes off, put a blanket on her, and reclined back into the chair, deep into the warm cocoon. Her tiny snores floated in the air.

I opened my eyes to Tony's hand on me. "Downstairs. Come on." He kept pulling until I got up. He grabbed the stuff. "Come on." Rachel went past me into the room, not saying anything.

Wasn't happy about being dragged from the warmth. I held on to the rail while going down the stairs and followed him into the kitchen. Tony and Rachel didn't want me enjoying the smack. They didn't want Chloe to enjoy it. Danny made a bitter, stomach-turning tea and threw me a scowl, worse than the smell.

Tony sat across the kitchen table and punched out his question. "Did you fuck her?"

That hurt somewhere. "No. She nodded off. I just took off her shoes and put a cover on her."

"Why'd you give it to her, you stupid fucking asshole?"

The whole lodge was upset with me, and my best friend was totally ape-shit mad. Had to be straight with them. "We were talking about different drugs on the way back from the beach." Tony had the meanest stare I'd ever seen. "She asked if I'd ever done smack. I told her I had some, and she wanted to try it."

"That doesn't mean you have to give it to her, you fucking moron." He kicked my chair. "Where'd you get the smack, asshole?"

I was getting tired of the name calling. "I ended up with a balloon from the party with Jack's chicks. Found it in my jacket."

"You ended up with one? What the fuck does that mean? You didn't know you had it? What bullshit!"

I started to explain, but I only had flimsy words.

"That stuff is poison, and you know it. I've seen people go down the toilet after playing with it. You fucking risked a good chick getting strung out. For what? Didn't think she'd fuck you?"

I was sobering up, sort of, from all the yelling and insults. "Look, she's a happy chick. She's not depressed. She wouldn't get strung out."

"Not depressed. Not fucking depressed? We're all fucking depressed. Why the hell do you think we're here? Because we were depressed back in the straight world? You think this is better? Is it? We have fun, but is it any different from our parents boozing up? Maybe we see things clearer, but seeing this shitty world clearer isn't any cure for depression. And you—you fucking idiot—you've been depressed for so long, you wouldn't know any different."

The bitter words and rank tea took over my stomach, and I lurched for the bathroom. Came out later to an empty kitchen and an empty living room, and I crashed on the sofa, defeated by myself. Defeated by aimless pleasure.

Last run

Tony and Chloe had gone off somewhere together or maybe separately. Rachel and Danny were at the lodge, but they ignored me. I was still raw from Tony's harsh lashes with the truth. I didn't want this life anymore and knew I had to close it down. I could have gotten a message through to the chemists, even though I was supposed to see them today. Tried to talk myself out of going over to Berkeley, but I needed a clean ending.

Their new place in the Berkeley Hills hid behind a high, wooden fence. Through a gate stood a two-story, white house with a red tile roof. Francis led me into a room with a view of the bay and the Golden Gate. Julian sat on a sofa, drinking coffee. Newspapers were spread all around.

I sat across a low table from them and got to the point. "I'm sorry, but it's over for me."

Julian took in a breath and leaned forward. "Cutting the number of people wasn't about you."

"I get that. Just one of many reasons."

They studied me, and Francis asked, "And the other reasons?"

"The main thing is—Tony's quitting. Blake's bust freaked him. Narcs are going undercover, trying to buy big lots. Rip-offs almost every day. Besides, I have to go to college someday."

They seemed satisfied. I started to get up, but Julian motioned to wait. "We have one last favor…" He looked at Francis, who nodded.

Francis went into another room, returning with a shoebox. He placed it on the table, pulled out the side flaps, and opened the top. "Eric is out of town till tonight, and we're leaving this afternoon. We were hoping you could deliver this. There's three thousand in there." He paused. "And two one hundred packages for you. Could you do this for us?"

Damn. Another run. I couldn't care less about the two hundred but agreed because I didn't want to say no. This would be the end of it, though.

"Good! Eric will be home after eight."

I picked up the box and studied it. Before I could say anything, before I could change my mind, Julian held open a book satchel for the box. "It's Berkeley."

On the way home, I stopped at the general store in Lagunitas for groceries and got an unwelcome surprise—the lodge had run up a tab unknown to me. The owner and his wife stood there, waiting for me to do something. Paying wasn't low profile, but not paying was worse, so I paid as if I'd been meaning to all along.

No one was home at the lodge, so I pulled right up to the garage. Thought about leaving a note for Danny to talk about the tab at the store but then remembered I was in the doghouse. My cabin felt familiar, too familiar. Took the box out of the book bag, opened it, and stared at the tabs. Just because I couldn't say no, I now had one more run. Busied myself going through my books. At some point, I drifted off.

Loud guitar riffs ripped me from sleep. It was past seven, and the box with the tabs loomed on my writing desk. I avoided the lodge on the way to the Olds. It was blocked by three other cars. Had to go in now. I found Danny, and we went out to look.

"The Triumph at the end is Ron's. He's not going anywhere. He'll let you borrow it."

Ron tossed me the keys to the two-seater without a problem. He just wanted it kept locked because he had some cables in the jump seat. There shouldn't be any traffic, and I could be at Eric's in less than an hour. Sometimes, I loved to drive by myself, forgetting everything but the road ahead and the cars around me. Other thoughts would flit through, but when focusing on the road, I could let them go—just observe and keep moving.

I made the tunnels above Sausalito in about thirty minutes. The bridge and a howling wind welcomed the Triumph. Tried to hug the line of the right lane, giving me a cushion from the curb. But the wind was so strong that it pushed the little Triumph around and forced its way into every hole, every gap in the little roadster, chilling my fingers on the wheel. A couple of times, I drove with one hand, rubbing the other on my leg to warm it up.

Midway on the bridge, a Highway Patrol car settled in behind me. I realized I'd left the box with the tabs on the passenger seat. How stupid! I'd asked Ron where his registration was but didn't stow the tabs. Couldn't worry about it now, though. I just had to maintain. After the tollbooth, he flashed his lights, and I pulled over.

"License and registration." His flashlight beam went from the papers to me and then back to the documents. "This car isn't yours."

"Yes, Officer. Ron's a friend. He asked me to take these cables into the city for his band. He's sick, and I'm doing him a favor."

"Step out of the car, please."

I did and stood five feet away, looking back at him. He was almost as tall.

"I'm going to ask you to walk away from me, placing your heel to your toe. Understand?"

"Yes."

"Start."

I did that just fine.

"Turn around and do the same."

No problem at all.

"Stop."

The wind snapped at my jacket and pants. My ears were colder than my hands.

"Are you all right? It looks like something's the matter with you."

"I'm cold, Officer. The Triumph lets the wind in, and it's freezing out here. Otherwise, I'm fine."

The wind didn't bother him in his tightly closed jacket. It barely moved the sharp crease on the front of his trousers. "Doesn't the heater work?"

"It doesn't have one. It's for hardy Englishmen."

"Did you play basketball?"

"Basketball?"

"You're tall."

"Oh! Yeah, I did. Good defender. Couldn't shoot at all. Glasses. Says so on my license, Officer." I held my wire rims out toward him. "Pretty thick."

He didn't reach for them. "All right. You can get back in the car."

After I'd gotten in and closed the door, he peered in, holding out my license and registration. "What's in the box?"

I turned to look at it and turned back. "Ron said fuses and stuff. What about you, Officer?"

"What?"

"Basketball? You're tall too."

"Couldn't jump."

I laughed just the right amount. "Can I go now, Officer?"

He motioned me on.

Mother's training had kicked in. My breathing slowed, and my mind was on extreme danger alert. But once I was away from the patrolman, adrenaline flowed, and I didn't want it. Needed to be calm, so I could think. Headed the car onto Park Presidio. Drizzle turned to rain, and the Triumph got even colder. He hadn't told me why I'd been stopped. I hadn't done anything suspicious, unless it was trying to warm my hands. How could he even see that through the tiny rear window?

God, I was sweating. How could I be sweating when it was this cold? Maybe it was just condensation. Maybe they were following me. Maybe they just wanted to see what I had in the damn box. How would they know I had it? Maybe they didn't have a warrant. Not yet. I turned right, right again while using the side road, and then right again, so I could cross over Park Presidio. I didn't see them behind me, but it was dark, and the little back window didn't let me see much, certainly not enough to pick out an undercover car.

I couldn't go straight to Eric with someone following me. Or were they? Needed a legit detour and then I remembered the cables. I just needed a band, a band near Eric. Hell, there were more bands in the city than dealers, and any one near Eric could work.

Kept checking the mirrors, one of which was completely useless now with the back window steamed up. I headed down Stanyan, past the hospital and the Panhandle. Within a couple of blocks of Eric's place, I looked and listened for a band as if I were looking for parking. Then drums, jumbled vocals, and one hell of a bass. Struck by dumb luck! A band was practicing in the house next to where Carlos and Annie used to live. I parked, arranged the cables over my right shoulder, and grabbed the box. Couldn't tell if anyone was watching me, but maybe they were. I had to go through with it.

There was no buzzer, so I knocked and banged on the door. I realized they'd never hear me until they took a break. They had to pause sometime. The instant they stopped, I pounded. A sizable freak with big hair opened the door. Roadie and security rolled into one. He was expecting somebody but not me.

"Ron sent me with the cables."

"We don't need cables."

"You sure, man? Ron said it was this house."

"I don't know Ron, and we don't need any cables." He started to close the door.

I wondered what he did need. "Sorry, man. Must be some mix-up. But somebody needs these, and I'm just helping out a roadie. Can I use your phone?"

Some ray of cable-lugging solidarity glinted through him, and he pointed me to a phone in a room down the hall. I made a show of calling and getting the right address while he stayed at the doorway with his back to me, watching his band across the hall.

"Say man, I'm Jake." I held out my hand. He still didn't know what to make of me, but we shook hands.

"Phil."

"I'm supposed to be two streets that way." I pointed through his back door. "Mind if I go out the back? It's raining, and it'll save me having to go all the way around this long block."

He was puzzled but not hostile. "Out the back?"

"Just to go through. Friends used to live in this house. There was a latch and a gate built into the back fence, so the neighbors could get together in the backyards. I'll show you." Fuck if I knew if there was a gate or a latch, but there had to be some way through to the other side.

I had his curiosity, and the band could practice without him. I followed him down the hall, through the kitchen and utility area, and down the steps into the yard. I paused under an overhang before the yard as if bracing for the rain.

"Thanks for your help. Let me give you something."

He started to speak, but I handed him the cables. He took them instinctively but said, "I don't need cables."

"Just hold a second." I pulled open the box's side flaps and opened the top. His eyes bulged. I jammed the big package in my armpit, stashed one of the smaller bags in my jacket pocket, and left the other in the box.

"You're no roadie!"

I handed him the box. "But you've got a hundred tabs, unless they make you nervous."

He took the box.

I strode out to the back fence—wood slats and posts about four feet high. There wasn't a gate or a latch, but there were no problems on the other side. I walked back to puzzled Phil to get some room. Put the big package in my left hand, turned, and hit the fence running. Right foot high up, hand on top, and vaulted it. I landed fine in the new yard and sprinted to the side gate. It was unlocked. I put the large bag back under my jacket. Out on the street, I didn't see a soul and just moved along as fast as any reasonable person would in the cold and wet.

I took a little detour—a block beyond and doubling back. Eric answered the door almost as soon as I rang the buzzer. "Been expecting you." He kept his place nice and neat. He could have won the Haight-Ashbury good housekeeping award, had one existed. Off-white matte walls with a shiny enamel light red trim. We sat in the living room on either side of an official coffee table and under framed movie prints for *The Maltese Falcon* and the *Days of Wine and Roses*.

"Any trouble?"

"Don't think so. Parked blocks away and did some detouring on the way here." Now that I was here, there was no need to drag him into my silly paranoia. We were either in the shit or not. I put the big package on the table.

"Thanks, man. I really couldn't get over there today." He picked up the bag. "Three thousand?"

"That's what they said." I put the smaller bag down. "And a hundred for a reasonable price."

"So, are you done? I can work with your people?"

"I'm done. Do you want the hundred?"

"Sure! Hear about the busts today?"

"No. What happened?"

"Remember that cat trying to buy five thousand? He was the heat, and they popped the people he bought from." He ran through the list of who'd been busted. I knew a couple, but none were close.

"If people weren't greedy, they wouldn't have sold to the runt." I wanted to leave and stood up.

"A couple of chicks are coming over," he continued. "You're welcome to stay."

Tempting but I needed to feel what it was like to be free of all this, and for that, I had to get out of a house with three thousand tabs. "Another time. I've got a borrowed car to return."

Outside, the wind had let up, and the rain had turned to mist. I wished it was pouring and took my time walking, hoping the rain would cleanse me. It didn't, but still, I was released. Gloriously, gloriously, and undeniably, I was released.

Stared at a corner store for a while but didn't want anything. The memory of my paranoia and my stupidity for leaving the box on the seat jolted me back. Realized that if they were following me, they'd expect me to come out of the same house. Fuck. It didn't matter now, and I walked up to the car from behind. I couldn't see anyone watching and sat behind the wheel of the Triumph, feeling my lungs fill and empty and letting my mind clear.

I was hungry but didn't want to see anyone I knew, so I decided on some seafood at the wharf. Sclioto's was uncrowded, and ever-friendly Troy let me use the phone. I got through to Ron at the lodge. New cables were fine, as long as I was buying.

When I finished my call, Troy asked if I was alone and then motioned to two young women in a booth. They worked at the department store, City of Paris, and lived in his apartment complex. They'd like me to join them.

"Hi. I'm Mark."

Makeup and subtly curled hair gave them away. They were from a different planet, one not populated by college girls and hippie chicks. "I'm Jenna, and this is Sonia."

Mid-twenties maybe. They weren't twins but looked alike in so many ways with their rounded lively faces, pert noses, and narrow lips. I had to fix them in my mind—Jenna, brunette with hazel eyes, and dark-haired Sonia. As they talked, they made small, close hand gestures. They even sat close to each other.

"Have you ordered yet?" I asked.

"We decided to wait when we saw you, but Jenna wants cioppino, and I want petrale Dore."

I ordered sand dabs, and Jenna ordered a bottle of white and a large shellfish salad for the table.

Sonia leaned forward and dropped her voice. "Troy lives in the same apartment complex as us." She glanced at him standing by the bar. "Did you know he's queer?"

"Seems probable. Why?"

She kept probing. "Ever been with a guy?"

Jenna laughed and reached out to stroke my hand. "She's not always like this."

Troy poured wine and left without any comment from my provocateurs.

"Guys have been hitting on me since I was about fifteen, but no, it never interested me," I said.

"You never put a stop to it?"

"Couldn't stop going to libraries."

"Why do you think they had an eye on you?"

"Don't know, but one guy said I had a tight ass."

They laughed. Sonia's glass shook, and a little wine popped out. "You do!"

Troy set the salad down and left. Jenna took my plate and gave me a healthy portion but held it out, so I had to reach. She and Sonia ate off the serving plate.

"What do you do, Mark?" Jenna asked.

It wasn't a question a freak would ever ask or usually answer, but what the hell. "I'm retired."

Jenna laughed while Sonia held a crab leg on her fork, moving it in the smallest of circles, anticipating the taste. "From what?"

The trouble with this conversation was that they both had their eyes on me, and I could only take in one at a time. "I was a psychedelic revolutionary"—I took the last bite of salad—"…but I'm no longer active."

A busboy cleared the table, and Troy delivered the next course. He offered to debone my sand dabs, but I wanted to show off and keep them hot as I ate. Jenna's cioppino gave off little clouds of tomato and herb aromas. I followed her eyes as she separated crab and mussels from the shell and ate. I left their gaze for my sand dabs. Ran my knife down the middle of one, slid the top half off the bone, and tasted the warm crunch of sautéed breadcrumbs and sweet warm flesh.

They chatted quietly with each other. I didn't bother listening in, content with my sand dabs.

As we finished the entrées, Jenna asked, "Our car is getting fixed. Troy was going to give us a ride home, but he doesn't get off for a while. Could you give us a lift? We're just off the freeway in Tiburon."

I warned them of the Triumph's lack of heating, space, or any other comfort besides speed and thrill. They weren't worried. We settled the bill, and Troy got kisses from them and a tip from me.

Sonia squeezed into the jump seat. Jenna seemed fine enough in the front, but Sonia shivered. I stopped before we hit the bridge and lent her my jacket. The food and wine had stoked me, and even my hands weren't as cold as they'd been on the earlier trip across. Fog sprawled across the lanes, and we hugged the far right, going the limit on an almost empty bridge. We hurtled through the Waldo Tunnel, down the big hill beside Sausalito, and got off at the Tiburon exit. Their apartment was as described, close by the freeway.

Outside the car, Sonia made no move to take off my jacket. "Come in with us. You can freshen up."

She meant more than that. In the restaurant, on the bridge, and just minutes ago, I'd thought of joining them. That was what I'd been doing for months, months, and months. I knew though, it wouldn't change how I felt in the morning, and I just wanted to be by myself.

"Sorry. I can't tonight."

They ignored that with inviting smiles and sashayed to their apartment, Sonia with my jacket still draped over her shoulders. They didn't think I could say no.

Hell with the jacket. I didn't mind the cold anymore.

***

Days went by. No Tony. No Chloe. Rachel and Danny still ignored me. I walked in the forest, avoiding people, seeing myself, and being ashamed. I'd go down Spring Road and Lagunitas Road to the general store and the post office, letting the dogs bark and run at me all the way. Somehow, I needed them to snarl at me. I made a practice of the dog gauntlet, down and back the long road. Shepherds and mutts barking, springing, and threatening. Couldn't think while they were clamoring, but my head was clearer back at the lodge.

I'd been dancing so close to the line for so long that it was just what I did. Thrills and highs every day, knowing I could get away with it all. Focused and alert but dancing as much for pleasure as for danger. But when the devil in pedal pushers showed up, it was so easy to cross another line, one

I'd known about all along. Miranda and the smack. Chloe and the smack. I'd never felt so ashamed.

Talking with Chloe had relieved some of the pain. She was in a good place and so forgiving. But it wasn't enough. I needed Tony's forgiveness, but he'd turned his back on me and shunned me, leaving me to stew alone in regret. At times, my anger at him could almost overwhelm me, but my logic would intrude and throw the cause of all of this in my face. I couldn't shake the aching need for his forgiveness.

Maybe I could start forgiving, but that'd be a long list to go through.

Mother? There was just a blank there, an empty slot. Sometimes I thought I should have feelings for her. Most people had a file in their brain marked "Mother," and all these stories, memories, and feelings were stashed there and easy to recover. My file was empty. The only way to live with her was to burn the memories every day.

Clare? Those little hairs by her ears. Her freckles and her earnestness. Her flipping out after the accident. Why did she turn on me that day and blame me? It was just a stupid car accident. What would have happened if she hadn't? Would I have left school? She had tried to get me to focus on my future. She'd been good for me, but I'd buried her, just as I had with Mother. But Clare didn't deserve it. She was just a kid when it'd happened. It was Clare who I had to forgive.

Wrote and rewrote one simple letter. When I was done writing, I organized all my things. Finished going through my books but couldn't get rid of any. Had to keep all my shoes, boots, and, of course, my carton of raspberry pastilles. The writing desk and rugs could stay. They were too bulky to move. There wasn't much else I wanted to keep, just some old concert flyers.

A knock on the door and Rachel came in carrying a bowl of rice and summer squash.

I was so much more grateful for her being there than I was for the warm bowl. "Rachel, I really blew it. I'm sorry. I'm so ashamed."

"Ashamed? Well, that's good." She sat in my chair. Her face was nowhere near a smile, but the frown receded. "You've never asked why I'm out here, why I'm living at the end of the road." She didn't wait for me to say anything. "When I lived in the city, some people I knew got into smack. None of them could handle it. Stealing, cheating, and lying. Anything for the next fix. I couldn't stay near them. Most of them were good people, but the smack turned them into devils."

I wasn't hungry anymore and put the bowl down.

"Why'd you even bring that shit here?"

I told her about Miranda, scoring at the drive-in, all my recent screw-ups, finding the balloon in my jacket, and not throwing it away.

"Doesn't anything scare you?" she asked.

"Losing Tony as a friend."

"He's furious with you."

"How about Chloe?"

"I don't think she'll try it again. You talked with her, right?"

"Yes, we're okay."

She looked at all my stuff, neatly arranged. "You're leaving?"

"Time for me to go, Rachel. Going back to Tucson. May not be the best place, but it's cheap, and I could probably get into college there." I pulled some pages off my little writing desk and handed them to her. "Could you read this? It's short. It's for a girl I was close to in Tucson, until she flipped out over a car accident."

Clare,

I've learned a lot since I last saw you. I learned I have a good conscience, but it's not automatic. I have to think about what I'm doing. I've learned the pleasure of my senses, all of them, and how easily I can let myself go from one little joy, one little thrill to another. But it doesn't last, and I have to keep going, chasing. I learned that the worst feeling is shame. It gets inside you when you deserve it, and it's so hard to shake. I learned that what I want most is to be able to wake up and feel good about myself. To look in the mirror and feel good, not at the image but so that I can look back with no shame and no embarrassment. Just some mixture of pride and humility.

I remember the joy we had. But near the end, I was uncomfortable because there was another girl, and I didn't tell you. Maybe I was a coward, but I think it was because I didn't want to hurt you. I'm very sorry, and I hope you'll forgive me.

I remember the car accident and all that followed. I'd like to know that blaming me bothered you. I like to think you have good memories of me. I wish I had a letter from you after all this time, but most of all, I want to let you know I forgive you.

I'm coming back to Tucson. I don't know where I'll be yet, but I bet Threckel still runs the Oasis, and you could leave a letter with him.

Mark

Rachel dropped the letter, came across the room, and put her arms around me. No experience with a woman had ever felt finer than Rachel hugging me—that letter written and read.

Route 505

A few mornings later, Rachel and I drove to Berkeley in her newest possession, the Oldsmobile Starfire. She needed forms to reenroll at Cal, and I needed new wheels. We parked on Dwight Way across from two almost identical Victorians, and I wandered Telegraph Avenue while she went onto campus. Bought a few issues of *Ramparts* from Cody's to help my transition back into society, along with a used *Candide*. Tables all along the street sold political buttons. Most of mine had disappeared, so I bought a few and put on one that said Yankee Come Home.

I walked on some more, weaving in and out of students, runaways, hippies, revolutionaries, and hurrying straights. A commotion came my way—three good-looking chicks dressed in pots and pans. Pots and pans, sneakers, and nothing else. Shouting, jumping, and pointing. Pots and pans swinging and clanging. Couldn't make out what they were shouting. They didn't touch anybody until they got to me. Kissed me, caressed my ass, and felt me up. Satisfied, they continued toward campus, clanging and shouting all the way.

I stood there, speechless. Passersby laughed and pointed. A bearded man in a corduroy sport coat said, "Street theater. Women's liberation." He didn't wait for a reply and walked off.

I saw Rachel on the other side and crossed the street. "Mark, I just saw something totally far out. Three liberationists making a statement about women as objects and the oppression of domestic roles."

"Yeah, they drafted me into a bit part."

"What?"

I managed a grin. "They surrounded me and treated me like an object."

She laughed and put a hand through my hair. "What a drag to miss that." She started toward the car. "When you get old, you can reflect on all the chicks you had and say, 'Then there were these three on Telegraph.'"

"Maybe I will. Tell the other people in the old folks' home all about it." We started walking, and I asked, "If I come back in a year, will I see you running down the street in pots and pans?"

"We'll be on to something else by then."

"I'll have to come back for that."

We reached the car, and she drove south on Telegraph, saying, "You know, I grew up in Piedmont."

"Piedmont. Where's that?"

"Little town near here with lots of wealthy squares, surrounded by Oakland."

"What's a town doing inside a city?"

"We had our own schools and police."

"You were segregated?"

"Yeah, we were segregated all right."

"You going over there after dropping me off?"

"Thinking about it. To see my parents."

"How long has it been?"

"More than a year."

Wished I had talked with Rachel more at the lodge. All those months and I didn't know where she was from or much about her family at all, but that wasn't unusual for the life we led. We'd all been orphans. "Do they know where you are?"

"They know I'm alive but not where I am. I send letters to friends in school back East now and then. They mail them to my parents."

"Why are you thinking of seeing them?"

"I'm dropping you in Oakland." Rachel, who was almost always relaxed, suddenly wasn't. "They were shits, but I miss them."

I didn't miss mine and had no good advice for family reunions, so I shut up. She found the auto dealers on Broadway in Oakland, stopped in front of a Ford shop, and said, "I'm going to cruise around up there and decide whether to see them or not. Don't worry about your boxes of stuff. I'll mail them as soon as you get me your address."

I'd forgotten the most important thing. "Rachel, about Tony, about what happened… Please try and talk to him for me."

"You may have lost him." She looked away and then back. "I'll try."

"We were partners… We went through a lot together. I trusted him."

"He trusted you too, and you broke it. But I'll try."

We hugged, and I got out with my bag and bad memories. Sat on a bus bench for a while, trapped in regret.

My only good friend lost, and my confidence needed three protesting women to prop it up.

After a while, I started working the car dealers, but my heart wasn't in it. I ended up with a used gray Ford F100, which I was pretty sure I hadn't bought at a great price. I found an on-ramp for I-580 east, hit a big left curve by an old theater, and left the Bay Area behind.

***

Tucson was hot, but what did I expect in August? I found a shotgun apartment in a one-story adobe on Court near Franklin for forty-five dollars a month. Called the lodge right away and left my new address for Rachel.

Spent the rest of the first week setting up my place, waiting for the phone company, and making sure I could register for the fall semester. Thought about looking for new contacts for SDS but decided to wait until school started and see what other groups were active.

I avoided the Oasis for a week, wanting to avoid Mother, but the possibility of mail drew me there, and late one afternoon, I went and saw old Mr. Threckel. Turned out that I hadn't needed to wait; Mother had moved to San Diego. The Oasis itself hadn't changed. Threckel had less hair and a larger belly but the same old bemused look. "Kept your mail after your mom left. One of the letters, a good-looking girl dropped off last month. Said she'd gone to high school with you. Told her you'd be back some day for my hot showers."

I recognized Clare's handwriting. Her bold, unhesitant script.

I gave him my address and went back to my apartment. Poured some sun tea from a big jar and sat on the sofa in my front room, alone with the letters. Clare's was dated six weeks ago, well before I'd written my still-unsent one.

She'd thought so much about what she'd done. How she'd betrayed me. Blamed me. Until that day, nothing bad really had ever happened to her. She felt her whole life crumbling because of the accident. She'd had dreams of what she could do with her life and what we could do together, but the accident shattered all of it, and she'd just been trying to save herself.

"Suddenly, I wasn't myself anymore. I was some out-of-control child. And just as suddenly, I was this cold calculating…"

She was ashamed. She often didn't feel comfortable looking at herself. She knew she couldn't have a relationship with anyone until she'd repaired the damage she'd done. Maybe we would never happen again; maybe we would. She knew she'd hurt me, but she'd started dealing with the mess she'd made. She'd told her parents the truth. They were furious with her, and they felt horrible for me. They'd wanted to write me, but she'd told them that she had to talk with me first. She wondered if I hated her.

I let it all sink in. Hadn't I wanted this letter all those months ago? Having read her words, though, I didn't know what to feel, what to do. For sure, I could forgive, but could I connect with her? How would it be to sit next to her?

I needed a distraction and fiddled with the little TV I'd bought from the prior renter. All that was on was the police riot at the Democratic Convention in Chicago. They usually had the pigs beating Black people on TV. But these were mostly white people, and they were sure getting a beating. The whole world was watching. What a society we had. What a spectacle! It all took my mind off Clare, but I could just see the both of us there. Politics had brought us together in the beginning. Hell, she could be there right now. I turned the stupid thing off.

I finally had an address, but I didn't want to send my letter to her in Massachusetts and wait for a reply. I needed her phone number. Why hadn't she put one in the letter? I called directory assistance in Cambridge but no luck. Maybe she was in a dorm. She'd told her parents. Maybe I should go over there and find out where she was right now. Reread her letter. Then picked mine up. Read it. Then hers. Again and again. Felt somehow absolved and decided to get a good sleep before visiting her parents in the morning.

I woke up, feeling alive and ready. Showered and went over the letters again. Put on some fresh jeans and a T-shirt and reminded myself to buy a pair of shorts. Too damn hot here for long pants all the time. I opened the door, and the postal guy walked up with packages. He usually came around midday. This was awfully early. I reminded myself that there was nothing to worry about now. That life was over. The packages were from Rachel, which arrested any lingering curiosity about them.

I'd introduced myself to the postal guy a few days before in a sort of postal worker solidarity, but I couldn't remember his name. I felt like asking for it, but I was in a hurry. "I have to leave. Let's just put them inside the door."

His sandy hair was ruffled, and sweat already showed in the armpits of his uniform shirt. His hands shook while holding out a clipboard for me to sign. Poor guy needed to see a doctor. I gave him a scrawl, and he twitched away to his nearby truck. I locked the door and jumped in the Ford, intent on finding Clare.

I focused on driving—the road, the cars, the traffic signs, and nothing else. I wasn't calm, though. I was excited. No…it wasn't excitement. Agitation or maybe anxiety. Whatever I was feeling, it wasn't one of my normal states.

They'd repainted her house. The same off-white but they'd taken the wood trim down to bare wood and stained it. I knocked on the door and heard Professor E. calling. "Clare, could you get that?" Incredible! She was there! The door opened, and I watched as Clare's face cycled through shock, uncertainty, joy, anxiety, and maybe a little fear before resting in an uneasy smile.

I put a finger to my lips and pointed to the truck.

Still a quick study, she turned back inside. "Dad, it's for me. I'm going out for a bit."

We drove a few blocks and parked. I thanked God for bench seating as she slid over to me. We hugged. Hugged to remember, hugged to forget, and hugged for what was coming.

I started to pull out the letter I'd written her, but she was already talking. Her voice sounded confident at first, but her eyes betrayed her anxiety. "Mark, I need to talk to you about everything, but please not in the truck." Her voice faltered. "Let's go to Himmel Park. It's close. We can find some shade and privacy."

I drove, no longer focusing on every detail around me, just doing enough to get there. My mind was unsettled and unsure. We found a tree near a little rise west of the library and sat cross-legged, face-to-face. I offered her a raspberry pastille, and she shook her head but then changed her mind. I took one myself. There was hardly anybody around, just a couple of moms watching two kids play with a ball about twenty yards away.

Clare put a hand on my knee. "You read my letter?"

"And I came to find you."

"I need to tell you everything, even though you read it."

I wanted to hear her tell me. Wanted the words spoken.

"My whole life changed when that car flipped. Suddenly, I wasn't myself anymore. I was so out of control. So horrible and mean… I so clearly remember you trying every which way to reach out to me, to comfort me, and I failed us both. I betrayed you. I'm so sorry." She lowered her eyes and stopped but not for long. "I barely held it together the rest of senior year. I knew what I'd done, how I must have hurt you, and what a shit I was. All I could do was focus on school and cry."

She wasn't crying now though. No… No, she was, and I might, too.

She continued, "I was so relieved to go to college, where I thought I'd be a new person. That I'd forget. But I couldn't. I just threw myself at boys. Was so lost. Finally, I told Mom and Dad about the accident, told them the truth. After that, I felt I could write to you, but your mother was gone, and I had no idea where you were or how to find you."

Her freckles, her tears, and her pain held me until I had a memory of how I felt when she kicked me under the table once—to tell me I was being silly and to shape up. I remembered feeling even closer with that kick, even closer than when we'd made love.

I saw a little kids' ball roll by. Damn. I noticed everything. But I didn't turn my head away. I stayed with Clare's eyes and didn't have to think to say, "When things in my life would go to hell, I'd just get calm and logical. You weren't prepared at all."

Her tears flowed, and I moved close, putting my arms all around her. We stretched out on the ground, on our sides, still face-to-face. We were so close. I could feel her breathing. I tried to match her rhythm but just a little slower.

Thought I should tell my story, so I told her about dealing and life in the Haight.

She listened without interruption. Her breathing was now almost normal, and her eyes focused on me. "I pushed you into that. I did." Her lips tightened as her chin dropped.

I placed my palm under her chin and got her eyes back on me. "No, I chose. I walked right into it. But it's all over now."

"I'm so sorry for what I put you through." She tilted her head the way she did when she was thinking.

I thought I should finish confessing. "There were lots of girls. Lots. And there was this one. Her name was—"

She stopped me. "I don't want to hear about that, Mark. I don't. Maybe some other time."

I studied her face. There were tears but no movement to push me off a ledge, to scramble away. She may have even been moving closer.

"Mark, I keep thinking how our lives would have been so different if I hadn't flipped out that day. Hadn't blamed you."

"No, no, no. I didn't leave just because of you. I was barely keeping it together in school. The lies, the hypocrisy. And my mother!" I was right but wondered why I wouldn't let her take responsibility for what she did. Why was I letting her off the hook? But that was obvious. I'd never wanted to hurt her, and now I just wanted to soften the self-inflicted blow.

She wiped my tears, and we managed little smiles. I stroked her hair back away from her face, revealing those soft little hairs around her ears.

"You always liked those hairs."

"And I still do."

"You have to be one of the oddest guys around." She looked around the almost empty park and said, "Friends at college took acid and had a good time. I was going to, but someone said I shouldn't if I had something really painful on my mind. That's when I really started thinking about the accident honestly."

"So, it was good, even though you didn't take it."

"Oddly, yes. You did it a lot?"

"Thirty or so. Some trips were incredible. Hard to describe. Maybe I see the world clearer now. Connections. Didn't make me a perfect person, though. I still did things I shouldn't have."

"Would you take it again?"

"With someone special. In a special place. Maybe out in the desert or in the mountains. Not in my tiny apartment."

She nodded, looked around, and asked, "Can I see your place?"

"Sure."

As we walked to the truck, she said, "Mark, I have a lot of guilt. But far, far more than that, I have feelings for you. I always have." She reached out with her left hand and gently rubbed my shoulder.

I gave her forehead a light kiss and wondered if this was all going too fast. At the truck, I had an idea and asked, "Can I show you something first?"

Her yes came with a what's-he-got-up-his-sleeve look.

I parked downtown and walked to the Fox Theater, the old art deco building. We stopped in front, and she said, "This is where we had our first kiss." She linked her left arm with my right. "What did we see that night?"

"A western. I can't remember which one."

She laughed. "If you can't remember, we sure didn't see much of it at all."

We smiled with memories of necking in one of the back rows.

She asked, "Time to get the truck and go to your place?"

"Let's forget the truck and take a walk. It's only about seven blocks."

"Lead on," she commanded, and I obeyed.

We walked past the white stucco courthouse with the tiled dome, glittering in the August sun. At each stoplight and at each street crossing, we paused, took each other in, and remembered something much more than young love.

Two blocks away from my place, I stopped cold. A block and a half away, a plain sedan with two heads showing above the front seat sat, facing my apartment. It meant only one thing, and I went all quiet inside.

I pulled Clare gently to me and leaned my back against a parked van, sheltering us from the sedan's view.

Clare asked, "What is it?"

"I've got a problem. There's an unmarked police car watching my place, and I think I know why. It's very stupid. Can't believe how stupid. Two boxes came for me this morning. Mostly my clothes and books, but I wanted to see you, and I left immediately." I pulled out the tin of pastilles. "There are some of these in the boxes. But one of them has tablets in it. The chemists I knew once ran filler through the tablet machine to test it. I saved some of the blank tabs as a souvenir. It was stupid. My buddy Tony even told me so. They look just like LSD tablets. If the post office or the cops searched the boxes, they could be waiting there to arrest me."

"I thought you stopped…"

"I did. I did. And they aren't acid, but they'll think they are until they test them." I held her hands and looked her in the eyes, hoping this wasn't the Clare that turned on me. "Clare, I need you to do something. I know how smart and strong you can be."

She grabbed my arm as if to go. "We'll just go over there and clear it up." I liked her even more, but she had no street smarts.

"Trust me. We need to make sure you're not caught up in this, so you can help out. You won't be able to do that if you walk over there and get arrested." I handed her my tiny address book and pointed to an attorney's name. "Take the book and go to him. Please. It's just a couple blocks away. Don't leave until you talk to him or his partner. I don't know them, but they'll take the case. Tell him everything, especially that they're just filler powder run through the machine." I paused and put my arms on her shoulders before going on. "Clare, that's all the tears you get for now. Please. His office is just two blocks away on Pennington."

"Why won't you come with me to the lawyer?"

"If I do that, it'd be like an admission of doing something wrong. I'm going to my place because there's nothing wrong. No acid. No drugs." I paused and put my hands on her shoulders. "This is our best chance."

She tossed her head as if she was trying to shake off a wave of confusion and fear, gave me a kiss, and strode off.

I watched her go, hoping I had a partner again. I walked over to my place, not taking my time or hurrying in any way. Almost abreast of the unmarked car, I realized that unless they had completely cleaned the tablet machine, there could easily be residue on some or all the tabs. Shit! I wondered if I'd been totally careless and had left something else among my things—a joint in a shirt pocket or a tab in a jacket. I almost stopped walking, but it was too late. I'd just have to maintain and hope Clare would stay with me this time. I reached my place, put the key in the lock, and heard car doors open and slam shut.

Tucson, 1973

Out of downtown and eight blocks away from the second interview of the day, I reached my street and stopped to set down my briefcase and loosen my tie. Four years of college but would it all be wasted? I hadn't really minded my bust, the probation. I deserved it for giving someone smack, but would it ever end? I looked up to see Clare down the street, pulling into our driveway.

I hurried along with the excitement I still felt every time I saw her, even though it had only been a short absence. She saw me coming and put a finger to her lips. Anthony was asleep in his car seat, and I watched him breathe for a minute until I felt Clare by my side. "Mom said he'd been full of energy for much of the day. He fell asleep on the way home."

I whispered back, "I'll carry him in."

She nodded and went to open the door. The building was from the 1920s—single story with thick walls covered in stucco and four shotgun apartments. Ours was one of the middle two. We used the first room as a sort of living room and then came our bedroom, which was followed by a huge walk-in closet, a large bathroom, our kitchen, and the nursery.

Clare had the crib ready, and I held the car seat, so she could easily move him into the crib. So assured and gentle as she placed him down and put a light cover over him.

We hovered by the crib, holding hands and feeling his glow until we tiptoed out. In the living room, I asked, "How was your day?"

"Fine," she said before sitting on the arm of my chair and continuing. "Come on! Don't hold out on me. Good or bad?"

"A good one and a difficult one."

"Difficult one first."

"This is the one Professor R. set up. They had the form with the question: have you ever been convicted of a crime. I checked the box and took the form into the meeting with one of the partners. He said he'd talked about me with Professor R. He understood, but he'd talked it over with his partners, and they thought engineering was too conservative of a profession for someone with a mistake like mine, even though I was such an outstanding student. He was sorry. He wished me luck and, oddly, said if I started with another firm, they wouldn't use this information against them."

"Oh. He's not going to bad mouth the firm you join to clients."

"You got it. He found the moral high ground by promising to not do what he shouldn't."

Clare had a variety of looks to show displeasure, but the one she wore now wasn't exactly one of those. It mostly said to go on.

"The next one was very different. They didn't ask if I'd been convicted of any crime, just if I've ever been convicted of a felony."

Her eyes lit up. "That's the first one?"

I nodded and went on. "I interviewed with Peters. He's the head, but he consults with his partner on major decisions. We talked about where the profession was going and where he wanted his firm to go. He asked what most excited me in school and said he was jealous of my outstanding engineering prize because he'd come in second decades ago."

She slid off the arm and squeezed into the chair with me. "It was going well?"

"Yes, very well. At the end, he asked if there was anything else on my mind, and I told him I had a misdemeanor."

"You what?" She got out of the chair. "We agreed you wouldn't if they didn't ask. You know our money situation."

"I'm sorry, but… I meet so few really good men, and he seemed to be one." I reached out my arm, hoping to draw her back, but she only took one step and then stopped.

Her breathing was shorter, faster. Her eyes moved away from me and back again.

"He asked if it was anything violent. I said no. Anything involving money. I said no. He looked at me, and I wasn't sure what he was going to ask next, but I just told him. He sat there, thinking for a while, and then he said something like, 'I gave you the opportunity not to tell me, and you told me.'"

She came back, sat in the chair, and ran a hand through my short hair. "We agreed, you know."

"I know, and I'm really sorry, but I was there, and it seemed the right thing to do."

"Okay. You were there. What's next?"

"He was going to talk with his partner and get back to me."

"When?"

"He only said it'd be soon."

I slid a hand down her backside and angled toward her for a kiss, but she shook her head. "You were there, and I understand, but it still bugs me. We agreed you wouldn't mention it."

The phone rang, and she leaped for it. "Yes, this is the Stenruds," she said.

"Yes, this is his wife."

"Oh, Mr. Peters. He was just telling me about you."

"Yes, he's right here. Do you want to speak…?"

"Yes," she continued, "that would be lovely. The four of us? Yes."

She held out the phone for me with a glorious smile.

#

About the Author

Paul Justison dropped out of high school in 1966 and fled to Haight-Ashbury, spending most of the next two years there and in Marin County engaging in all the pleasures and follies that magical time had to offer. After the sixties ended, he went to college, started a career, and raised a family. He has been published in *The Rumpus*, *The Gambler Mag*, *Flash Fiction Magazine*, and *Fiction on the Web*. *Lost and Found in the 60s* is his first novel.

About the Press

Unsolicited Press was founded in 2012 and is based in Portland, Oregon. The press produces stellar fiction, nonfiction, and poetry from award-winning writers. Authors include John W. Bateman, T.K. Lee, Rosalia Scalia, and Brook Bhagat.

Find the press on Twitter and Instagram: @unsolicitedp

Learn more at www.unsolicitedpress.com.